The Un-Welcoming Party

Clint heard the faint sound of iron brushing against steel. Under normal circumstances, he might not have picked up on that sound. Since that sound now meant a gun was being drawn, Clint didn't have any trouble distinguishing it from the rest.

Reaching out with a speed that put the others to shame, Clint snagged the gun from the closest man's holster and took it away from him. With a flick of his wrist, Clint tossed the gun away and shifted his attention to the next man.

Behind Clint, one of the others balled up a fist and slammed it into the small of Clint's back. A sharp, stabbing pain exploded in Clint's innards, forcing him to clench his teeth and spin around before that pain got any worse.

Clint found himself face-to-face with one of the men who'd escorted him onto Walsh's property. Before, the man had been cold and aloof. Now, he wanted Clint dead. That much was made perfectly clear just by looking into his eyes and reading the hatred there. . .

. . . It was only a matter of time before the lead started to fly.

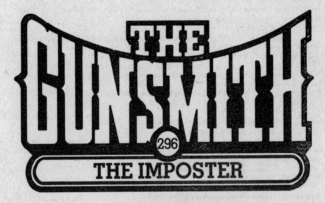

THE GUNSMITH

296

THE IMPOSTER

J. R. ROBERTS

JOVE BOOKS, NEW YORK

THE BERKLEY PUBLISHING GROUP
Published by the Penguin Group
Penguin Group (USA) Inc.
375 Hudson Street, New York, New York 10014, USA
Penguin Group (Canada), 90 Eglinton Avenue East, Suite 700, Toronto, Ontario M4P 2Y3, Canada
(a division of Pearson Penguin Canada Inc.)
Penguin Books Ltd., 80 Strand, London WC2R 0RL, England
Penguin Group Ireland, 25 St. Stephen's Green, Dublin 2, Ireland (a division of Penguin Books Ltd.)
Penguin Group (Australia), 250 Camberwell Road, Camberwell, Victoria 3124, Australia
(a division of Pearson Australia Group Pty. Ltd.)
Penguin Books India Pvt. Ltd., 11 Community Centre, Panchsheel Park, New Delhi—110 017, India
Penguin Group (NZ), Cnr. Airborne and Rosedale Roads, Albany, Auckland 1310, New Zealand
(a division of Pearson New Zealand Ltd.)
Penguin Books (South Africa) (Pty.) Ltd., 24 Sturdee Avenue, Rosebank, Johannesburg 2196,
South Africa

Penguin Books Ltd., Registered Offices: 80 Strand, London WC2R 0RL, England

This is a work of fiction. Names, characters, places, and incidents either are the product of the author's imagination or are used fictitiously, and any resemblance to actual persons, living or dead, business establishments, events, or locales is entirely coincidental.

THE IMPOSTER

A Jove Book / published by arrangement with the author

PRINTING HISTORY
Jove edition / August 2006

Copyright © 2006 by Robert J. Randisi.

ISBN: 0-515-14174-7

JOVE®
Jove Books are published by The Berkley Publishing Group,
a division of Penguin Group (USA) Inc.,
375 Hudson Street, New York, New York 10014.
JOVE is a registered trademark of Penguin Group (USA) Inc.
The "J" design is a trademark belonging to Penguin Group (USA) Inc.

PRINTED IN THE UNITED STATES OF AMERICA

10   9   8   7   6   5   4   3   2   1

ONE

"Get the hell off my property."

No matter how forcefully the slender man talked, he wasn't able to budge one of the intruders who'd caused him to come out to the barbed-wire fence. That fence hung in tatters here and there as cows shuffled back and forth, completely oblivious to the bad intentions filling the dry air.

The man who'd spoken was a lean figure in a suit that was out of place in the middle of the New Mexican emptiness. While not exactly in the desert, the land had the wide-open feel of a desert with a few scattered clumps of bushes and trees.

"In case you didn't hear me," the man repeated as he stood up in his cart and raised his voice, "I just asked you men to leave."

Spread out in front of the man's cart was a row of half-dozen riders. They all sat easily in their saddles as if they were just out there to take in a quiet sunset. A few of them glanced in toward the middle of the line where a stocky man in his late thirties sat upon a dark gray horse.

"We heard what you said, Englishman," the stocky man replied. "But that don't mean we need to jump."

The man in the cart scowled a bit and adjusted his coat.

1

When his hands went anywhere close to the gun strapped around his waist, all the riders in front of him slapped their hands onto their own firearms.

"No need for all of that," the man in the cart said. Now that he'd lowered his voice, the English accent was easier to make out. "You men are on my property and I'm asking you to leave."

"You sure sound a lot more courteous now. Maybe you finally see that you're outnumbered."

"Come now, Martin. This doesn't need to come to blows."

"If you mean me blowing that head clean off yer shoulders," the stocky man replied, "then I gotta tell you the thought crossed my mind once or twice."

"Just take your men back across my fence and there won't be a problem."

"What about these cows? They're mine."

"Take them with you, then, Martin."

"That's Mr. Walsh to you." When he said that, his eyes narrowed as he carefully studied the Englishman's face.

Although he paused for a few moments to take in a breath or two, the Englishman finally nodded. "Fine, Mr. Walsh. Take your animals and get off my property."

"That's better."

Seeing the smirk on Walsh's face, the other riders seemed more than a little disappointed that there wasn't going to be a fight any longer.

"Gather up them cows," Walsh said, dashing the hopes of the last few riders. Stabbing a finger toward the man in the cart, he added, "And you'd better not pull any more shit with this fence or there'll be hell to pay."

Obviously offended by that remark, the Englishman straightened up and said, "I beg your pardon? You were the one to cut that fence! Either you or one of those thugs you call ranch hands."

Walsh glared at him as if he'd just been punched in the

face. "Why the hell would I cut my own fence? You think I want to see my livestock cross onto your land so you can steal them out from under me?"

Sensing the growing hostility the way a shark senses blood in the water, Walsh's men gathered around him once more. Only one of them bothered tending to the cows any longer. The rest of the men were grinning and waiting for a reason to draw their weapons and get to work.

The Englishman shifted nervously in his seat and looked over both shoulders. At the last second, he spotted what he'd been searching for and let out the breath that had been stuck in the back of his throat. As he turned to look back in Walsh's direction, a trio of riders drew up alongside the cart.

"What's the problem, Mr. Livingston?" one of the new arrivals asked.

Not only Walsh, but every one of his men eyed the man who was now drawing up next to Livingston's cart. Although the tension was still in the air, the original set of riders no longer seemed so eager to fight.

"Just a little dispute over a broken fence," Livingston said.

"The fence was cut," Walsh grunted. "Probably so you could get us all here and riled up so your gunfighter there could finish us off."

The man next to Livingston shifted his eyes toward Walsh in a way that put a chill in the air between them. He leaned forward a bit in his saddle in a way that made it feel as if he'd stepped right up to stand in Walsh's face.

"Rotten talk like that is what causes folks to get so riled up," the new arrival said.

Although he'd lost a bit of the edge in his voice, Walsh still held his ground. "We ain't afraid of you. Just because that Englishman can hire The Gunsmith don't make him right in this matter. It just means he's got enough money to get another killer on his side."

"Is that so?"

"I said it, didn't I?"

Nodding, the gunman pulled back on his reins so he could put a few steps between himself and Walsh. His hand drifted toward the Colt around his waist and his gaze turned into a steely glare. "Which one of your men cut that fence?"

"None of them," Walsh replied. "It was that Englishman's doing."

As soon as those words were out of Walsh's mouth, Livingston pointed to the man at Walsh's left and said, "Probably that one there. He's been snooping around my land before."

Without a moment's hesitation, the gunman drew his Colt and put a bullet through the skull of the man Livingston had pointed out. The shot cracked through the air and was followed by the heavy thump of a body hitting the dirt.

"There now," the man called The Gunsmith said. "Dispute settled."

TWO

There was a couple moments of silence, but not out of respect for the newly deceased. Instead, the other men were shocked beyond reason at the gruesome spectacle they'd just witnessed. When that passed, Walsh and every one of his men went for their guns.

Since they were all mounted, Walsh and his men weren't able to get their pistols from their holsters as quickly as they wanted. It was only a difference of less than a second, but that was more than enough time for the man who'd fired the first shot to pick his next target.

The Gunsmith's pistol barked once more, taking a piece of meat from another man's side. Walsh wasn't the man who caught the lead, but he scowled as if he could feel it all the same. Lead filled the air like rain as thunder rolled in from all those smoking barrels.

Despite the gun at his side, Livingston was huddled down in his cart with both arms covering his head. He gritted his teeth and clenched his eyes shut, praying for the fight to be over but also anticipating the worst.

Walsh had his sights on The Gunsmith, but shifted them when he saw he was about to be shot by one of the other

5

men who'd come to Livingston's side. One pull of the trigger was all it took for him to drop Livingston's man from his saddle. No matter how much noise was swirling through the air, Walsh could hear his bullet punch through the other man's chest.

"Move them back!" Walsh shouted to his men. "Do it, now!"

Reluctantly, the men complied and the gunshots tapered off. From there, they moved their horses back a few paces and turned to make sure they wouldn't get shot in the back.

"You got what you wanted?" Walsh asked. "You spilled some blood and drove us off. That make you feel like a big man?"

Livingston didn't respond. He was just starting to peel his arms away so he could look at what was happening. There was no way he could hide the fact that he was shaking like a leaf.

"Just get off my property," Livingston said. "That's all I ever wanted."

Walsh nodded as he motioned for his men to head for the break in the wire. "We both lost a man, but that hired gun of yours fired first. You can bet your ass the law will hear about that."

"Tell the sheriff what you will. He knows well enough that you're far from innocent in all of this."

Walsh kept nodding as he snapped his fingers to catch a few of his men's attention. Pointing to the animals that were running from the gunshots, he said, "Gather up them animals. You better not lift a damn finger, Englishman, even if one of them cows jumps onto your front porch."

"Take them and go," Livingston said in a shaky voice. "I don't want any more bloodshed."

"Yeah," Walsh grunted as he looked at the smirking gunman who'd fired the first round. "Sure you don't."

•   •   •

About half an hour later, the cows had been rounded up and were being moved through the gap in the broken barbed wire. Walsh watched every second from a spot several yards into his own property. This time, a rifle was resting across his lap and an angry scowl was etched into his face.

One of his men rode up to him and came to a stop. "That's the last of 'em."

"You sure about that?"

"Yes, sir, Mr. Walsh. We counted."

"Count them again. And I mean all of them. I want every head of cattle accounted for. It's just that Englishman's style to steal a few head while we were all distracted out here."

The man nodded and snapped his reins as a younger fellow carried a toolbox out to mend the broken wire. Although the youth was skilled at his work, it was obvious that he was rushing in order to be done as quickly as he could manage.

For a few minutes, Walsh and the other man stood by and watched the younger one patch the wire. Even though their eyes were pointed in the general direction of the fence, it was easy enough to see they weren't watching it too closely.

Finally, the man next to Walsh cleared his throat and asked, "What are we going to do about what happened?"

Walsh let out a breath, which seemed to be the only thing keeping his head up. "Was it Davis that was shot?"

"That's right."

"He wanted to lock horns with one of those Englishman's boys for a while. I guess he got his wish."

"You don't seem too sorry about it."

"Being sorry won't change nothing," Walsh replied as he shot a sideways glance to the other man. "What I'm sorry about is that I need to hire gunhands rather than cowboys anymore. You recall them days when all we worried about was moving cattle from one spot to another?"

"Yeah. It wasn't long ago."

"Feels like it's been a goddamn lifetime." Walsh filled his lungs and let another breath out. This time, he was able to sit up straight once more when he was through. "You know who it was on our side that made a kill?"

"Pardee, I think."

Walsh nodded. "If we take this to the sheriff, then the Englishman will probably insist that he be arrested as well. Pardee's a good man, but he was bound to kill someone sooner or later. Handing him over might be a good thing."

"Or we might need him if things get uglier. Especially since that Englishman's got The Gunsmith working for him. Do you think that was really him?"

"He's a hell of a shot and that's all that matters. Once the blood starts to pour, names don't count for much anyhow. By the looks of it, plenty of blood is gonna flow before this is done."

THREE

Livingston drove his cart just out of view of the broken spot in his fence. From there, he watched Walsh's man fix the wire. Only after Walsh's entire party had left the area did Livingston put away his spyglass and snap his reins.

"You want me to go finish them off?"

Glancing over to the gunman who'd asked the question, Livingston shook his head. If the question had come from anyone else, he might have thought they were joking. From this man, however, Livingston didn't know quite what to expect.

"No need. I think we've done enough," Livingston said.

The man beside Livingston's cart shrugged. He was tall and had a face covered in scars. Dark hair covered his scalp and face, making it look like the shadows were sticking to him. "Whatever you say."

"Those men knew who you were."

"Plenty of people know who I am."

"I suppose The Gunsmith is something of a legend in these parts."

"Yeah. You suppose right."

Livingston's cart was moving along at an easy roll, covering land that he knew like the back of his own hand. It was a good thing the Englishman didn't have to watch where he was going, because his attention was focused on other things. The more he focused on them, the tighter the knot in his stomach became.

"That man you, ah, shot," Livingston stammered. "Did you know him?"

"All I know is he's dead." The gunman studied his employer carefully. "What's the matter? You getting squeamish?"

"I had hoped to avoid bloodshed if necessary."

The gunman laughed. "That ain't what you said when you hired me."

"I know."

"Just go back to your big ol' house and have something to eat. Have yourself a drink and enjoy that wife of yours. That ought to take your mind off of things. Leave the rest to me."

The third man who'd come to Livingston's side approached quickly. His horse thundered up alongside the cart and slowed to match the others' pace. Judging by the way the rider was huffing, one might have thought he'd run all that way on his own.

"I got him," the third man said, nodding over his shoulder.

Draped over the back of the third man's horse was a bundle that looked like a thick carpet that had been rolled up and dropped behind the saddle. The feet sticking out of one end were hard to miss, and so was the top of the dead man's head, which protruded from the horse blanket in which the body had been wrapped. Although the gunman barely gave the bundle a glance, Livingston couldn't seem to take his eyes off it.

"Take a good look at that dead man," the gunman said under his breath. "Think about that when you start to feel bad about the rest."

Livingston's eyes narrowed and he nodded solemnly. "That Irish son of a bitch has gone too far. I knew he'd be trouble when I first met him. It wasn't long after that when he started trying to carve off pieces of my property."

"Where should I take him?" the third man asked, gesturing toward the dead man.

"Take him into town," Livingston replied. "Show him to the sheriff before taking him to the undertaker."

The gunman cleared his throat in a way that made it clear what he thought about that decision.

"What's the matter?" Livingston asked.

Shrugging, the gunman said, "If you want to trust some lawman with your affairs, that's your choice. I just figured you hired me and the others to take care of things for you. Lord knows they'll get done a lot faster that way."

The third man was the youngest, and he looked back and forth between Livingston and the gunman like a child waiting to see which parent would overrule the other.

"You know the law might look at you just as hard as they'll look at Walsh," the gunman said casually.

"Would that be a problem?" Livingston asked.

The gunman's only response was a glance and half a smirk.

"Yes," Livingston said. "I see your point." Looking over to the younger man carrying the body, he said, "Take him to the undertaker. If anyone asks, just tell them it was an accident."

"All right, Mr. Livingston."

"You made a good choice there," the gunman said. "No need to make this into a bigger mess than it already is."

"You'd better be able to wrap this up," Livingston said as he focused his full glare onto the gunman riding beside him. "I paid good money for you and I expect it to be worth my while!"

"You wanted the best, that's what you got. Anyone will tell you The Gunsmith is the best there is."

Livingston nodded slowly. "I didn't think I'd lose any more men once you were in my employ."

"Then maybe you should let me bring in my own men. The ones you've got here barely know which end of a pistol to point away from themselves."

"Your own men? You mean more hired gunfighters?"

"I ain't talking about farmers," the gunman replied. "The right kind of help is always what you need to get any job done. This one ain't no different."

"I suppose these men will cost me more money?"

"Should come out even if you factor in all the coffins you'd need to buy for these boys working for you now. Or you may be ahead if that Irishman winds up rolling straight over you."

That set off a spark inside Livingston that a blind man could have spotted. "Send for a few of these men, but I'll want to speak to them before they're hired."

The gunman tipped his hat and flicked his reins. He steered toward the north and rode away.

FOUR

Emmett Livingston's spread was fairly impressive. Like the proverbial diamond in the rough, his house was an elegant structure complete with a decorative fence nestled in the middle of a sprawling stretch of hard New Mexican land.

The house was two floors high and resembled something out of a painting. In fact, it might have been more at home on a plantation somewhere in the Carolinas. Even the gunfire from the previous day wasn't enough to spoil the atmosphere of that house. The single rider approaching from the west took his time and rode at an easy pace. He looked from side to side, taking in the sights until he got to the pretty wooden fence.

Dismounting, the rider tied his horse to a brass ring set into an oak post and pushed open the delicate little gate. Compared to the quaint surroundings, the man with the thick beard carrying the shotgun seemed more than a little out of place as he came running down the front walk.

"Who're you?" the man with the shotgun asked. "What're you doing here?"

Perhaps due to the peacefulness of the house in general, the stranger didn't even make a move for the gun at his

13

side. He stopped short and looked at the man with the shot-gun the way he might regard an odd cloud formation. "I'm here to see Emmett Livingston. Isn't this the right place?"

"Mr. Livingston?"

"That's the one."

"Is he expectin' you?"

"I don't know, but I do know that shotgun isn't necessary."

The man glanced down at his hands as if he'd forgotten about his shotgun. Seeing the weapon gave him a boost of confidence, however, which lasted right until he got an-other look at the stranger's steely eyes. "I'll go fetch Mr. Livingston. You stay right here!"

The stranger held up his hands as if the other man's tone had an effect on him. He stayed put and patted the neck of his dark horse.

Dashing back into the house, the man with the shotgun reappeared a few seconds later. This time, he was accom-panied by the slender Englishman. Livingston appeared tired, which made his skin a little paler and his hawk nose stand out a bit more.

"I'm Mr. Livingston. What can I do for you?"

The stranger kept one hand on his horse and used the other to casually tip his hat. "My name's Clint Adams. The real Clint Adams, that is."

Livingston's expression froze as if it had been carved onto his face forever. It slowly shifted as he took in the sight of the man in front of him. The longer he looked, the more he shifted on his feet. "I assume you can prove your claim?"

Clint smiled. "It's funny that you want me to prove my-self, but didn't flinch before hiring some gunman claiming to be me."

"You seem to know a lot on this matter."

"I've been spending some time in these parts. You could imagine my surprise when I heard I was being known for gunning down ranch hands outside a town I never even heard of. Luckily for me, the U.S. marshals in Lincoln County check on their facts a little better than you do."

Although Livingston seemed put off by those words, he couldn't exactly refute them. Instead, he huffed a bit and then motioned for Clint to follow him. "Come inside, Mr. Adams. That is, if that's who you truly are."

Clint walked up to the porch. His hands hung at his sides within easy reach of his modified Colt, but not close enough to ruffle any feathers.

"You come along, too," Livingston said to the man with the shotgun. "And don't speak a word of this to anyone. At least, don't mention anything about who this man claims to be."

"All right, Mr. Livingston."

Livingston opened the front door to his house and waited for Clint to pass.

The inside of the place was every bit as refined as the outside. Elegant furnishings sat on top of expensive carpets. Fresh flowers were displayed in crystal vases, giving the air a sweet scent. Just walking into the place was enough to make Clint wish he'd bathed before paying Livingston a visit.

"Nice place you have here," Clint said.

"It's not much, but it's home," Livingston replied.

"Take it from me. It's plenty. Then again, I've been sleeping on the ground for the last three nights."

Livingston chuckled under his breath, which was enough to loosen him up just a bit. "Can I offer you some refreshment?"

"Water would be fine, thanks."

Livingston looked over to make sure one of the servants heard the request. When he saw the young girl hurry off to the kitchen, he settled into a luxuriously padded chair. "What brings you here, sir?"

"I don't think you forgot already."

"Ah, yes. You claim to be Clint Adams?"

Clint nodded. "I do. In fact, I'd like to meet the other man making that claim."

"That might not be such a good idea."

"Why not?"

Letting out a measured sigh, Livingston said, "Because I already know how that conversation would go. What exactly is your intention in coming here? Surely someone taking your name for a bit isn't causing that much harm."

"I've had men claim to be me in order to get invited to some high-stakes card games in San Francisco. I've even had some men do that to impress a lady. When they use my name so they can get away with murder, it cuts a little deeper."

Clint leaned forward with his hands clasped and his eyes fixed upon the Englishman. "I've used my gun on plenty of occasions and accept the responsibility. I will not, however, accept the responsibility for a murderer who shoots off his mouth as much as he shoots off his gun. Some lawmen aren't as partial to reason as the marshals in Lincoln County."

"Point taken," Livingston said with a weary nod. "I'll have a word with the man in my employ who has taken your . . . that is . . . who also claims to be this Gunsmith fellow."

"If it's all the same to you, it would be quicker if I just had a word with him."

Livingston raised his hands. "I wasn't looking for any Gunsmith when I hired him. If he knows that, he may just choose another name and go from there. I'd rather not have any more frayed tempers around here if I can help it. There's been more than enough violence of late."

"Is that so?"

"Most of it comes courtesy of my neighbor, but yes. There's been more blood spilled lately than I care to think about."

"Shouldn't you expect as much when you hire gunmen?

Even if their names aren't mine, they still have a penchant for using their iron."

"It's a long story, but I assure you that hiring those men was a last resort. In fact, I may have to let some of them go. After all, if I can't even trust them when they tell me who they are, how can I be certain they're on the straight and narrow about anything else?"

"Good question."

"You look tired, Mr. Adams. It's late and it will be dark before you can ride back into town. Since you came all this way, why not stay the night?"

"If that won't be an imposition," Clint replied.

Livingston waved that off quickly. "Not at all. Please, make yourself at home."

FIVE

This wasn't the first time that someone had taken Clint's name to suit their own purposes. Most of the time, it was tossed about in saloons even more than predictions about the weather. And most of the time, Clint himself didn't mind.

Men who wanted to pose as The Gunsmith were usually after some bit of fame or recognition. Unfortunately, there were enough gunmen out there looking to make a name for themselves that those imposters always had someone to call their bluff. And, even more unfortunately for them, that bluff was usually called in a hailstorm of lead in the middle of a street.

Clint chose his life and accepted the bull's-eye on his head that came along with it. Anyone who was stupid enough to want that same bull's-eye on themselves deserved whatever came to them. This time, however, was a different story.

This time, the man who'd taken his name was hiding behind it so he could kill with reckless abandon. That sort of thing attracted attention from the law. If it went on too much longer, the fire might get too high for it to be put out before Clint found himself at the end of a noose. That's what brought him to Livingston's house, and that's why he'd decided to stay the night.

In the short time he'd spent with the Englishman, Clint was hard pressed to say whether or not Livingston was hiding anything. There was clearly plenty going on, but nobody was even trying to hide that much. Under those circumstances, the man who'd taken Clint's name would either give up the charade without much fuss or come knocking on Clint's door to have it out face-to-face.

Either way, Clint was ready for it.

Until that second shoe dropped, he figured he might as well keep his eyes and ears open while enjoying Livingston's hospitality. The room Clint was shown to was on the second floor at the middle of the hall. Livingston had said his farewells without going up the stairs, allowing one of his hired hands to show Clint to his room.

"Think I could get a room at the end of the hall?" Clint asked.

The hired hand was a boy not even in his teens. By the looks of him, he was a local kid from a poor family. His cheeks were a little too sunken and his eyes were a bit too wide for him to have been raised in that castle of a house.

For a moment, the kid didn't know how to respond. His eyes darted from the door he'd been instructed to open to the one at the farthest end of the hall. "Umm . . . I was supposed to take you to this room. Mr. Livingston says so."

"Is there anyone in that room?" Clint asked, pointing to the end of the hall.

"Well . . . not that I . . ."

Just then, the door that both of them were looking at opened and a dark-haired woman stepped through it. She wore a simple dress and had her arms full of bundled sheets.

"Is anyone sleeping in that room?" the kid shouted down the hall.

The woman shrugged and shook her head. "No. I just stripped the linens, though."

Hooking a thumb toward Clint, the kid said, "He wants to sleep there instead of here."

"I don't see the difference," the woman said. "All of these are guest rooms and he looks like a guest, so he can take his pick."

The kid looked back to Clint, and then shrugged and started walking down the hall. Clint followed, and stepped aside to let the dark-haired woman pass. She was slender and had smooth, pale skin. She also was in a hurry because Clint didn't get a chance to see much more than that before she was heading back down the stairs.

Pushing open the door, the kid walked inside. "Here you go. It's just the same as all the rest, so I don't know what the fuss is about."

"It's bad luck to sleep so close to the stairs," Clint said.

"Really?"

"No, but it is a bit quieter."

The kid rolled his eyes and grinned. That smile, along with his eyes, grew even wider when he spotted the silver dollar Clint was handing over to him.

"Thanks for the help, kid. Take this and get yourself some candy."

"Gee, thanks!"

"Before you do that, do you think you could bring my saddlebags up here?"

"Sure!"

"There's another dollar in it for you if you're the one who watches after my horse."

"Mr. Livingston's got men who do that stuff," the kid said with disappointment.

"I'll bet he does. I want you to do it for me, though. Do you know how to take care of a horse?"

Nodding vigorously, the kid said, "My ma's got six horses at home and I can saddle up every one of them. She says I'm better than my older brother at it, too."

"Then I made a good choice," Clint said. "I'll pay you a

dollar a day to look after my horse. His name's Eclipse. I'll also pay extra for you to let me know if anyone comes snooping around him or if anyone asks about me."

The kid scowled a bit at that.

"You look like you see a lot," Clint said in a more confident tone. "I'll bet you see more than most anyone could guess."

"Yeah. I suppose."

"Then you know about all the commotion that's been going on around here."

All Clint needed to see was the shadow that came over the kid's face to know he'd hit the nail on the head.

"I just want to make sure there's no more trouble on my account," Clint said. "If you don't hear anything, I'll still pay you for your trouble. Is it a deal?"

Shrugging, the kid stuck out his hand. "Deal."

SIX

Not even fifteen minutes went by before the kid came knocking on Clint's door. Actually, he knocked once before pushing open the door and trudging inside. He had Clint's saddlebags draped around his neck and was lugging them like an ox with a yoke over his shoulders.

"That's a real nice horse, mister."

"The name's Clint."

"I think he likes me, too. He liked the sugar cubes I gave him, that's for sure. Here's your bags," the kid said in a rush as he dumped the saddlebags next to the door. "Oh, and someone was asking about you."

Clint narrowed his eyes and aimed them straight at the kid. "Really? That was awfully quick."

The kid held up under that scrutiny for all of three seconds. After that, he let out a breath and said, "Actually, it was only Meredith who asked about you. She asks about everyone."

"Was Meredith the one who was coming out of here before? The one with all the sheets in her hands?"

"Oh, no. That was Claudia. She works here like me. Meredith is Mr. Livingston's wife. She says she wants to meet you."

"Did she ask you or was she talking to someone else?"

"Someone else. I was walking by, so I didn't see who it was. After I was done putting Eclipse into the stables, I tried to go back and see who it was, but they were gone."

Clint fished some money out of his pocket and handed it over. "Here you go, kid. Nice try."

But the kid shook his head as if he was embarrassed. "No, sir. That wouldn't be right. Like I said, Mrs. Livingston asks about everyone."

Nodding, Clint tucked the money back into his pocket. "Honest men go a long way. What's your name?"

"Will."

"Keep your ears open, Will. I pay better now that I know you're playing straight with me. In fact, take this anyway," he said while offering the same money that had already been refused. "Consider it a bonus for taking such good care of Eclipse."

This time Will took the money eagerly. "Thanks, mister!"

"I told you, it's Clint."

"All right, Clint. Thanks!" Will turned and started to run out of the room, but stopped with his hand still on the door's handle. "Oh, Mrs. Livingston will be wanting to talk to you. She said she wanted to pay you a visit real soon."

"Okay. I'll keep my eyes open for her."

With his message delivered, Will left the room so quickly and slammed the door so hard that it swung partly open behind him.

Clint stepped over to the door, shaking his head. The last time he'd run that fast was when his life had depended on it. Even then, it barely seemed worth the effort.

Just as Clint was pushing the door shut, he heard someone else step up to it and push it open from the hall. The noise from the kid's hasty departure had been enough to cover those other footsteps until just this moment, and Clint was barely quick enough to keep from being knocked in the face by the door as it was opened again.

"Oh, sorry about that," the dark-haired woman said as she saw how close she'd come to pushing the door right into Clint's face. "I thought you'd gone."

"Nope," Clint replied. "Just watching that boy run like that is enough to tire me out."

She smiled through the crack in the door and held up the load in her arms. "I brought some fresh sheets. Mind if I come in?"

"Oh, certainly," Clint said. It was only then that he realized he was still holding the door, preventing it from opening. "You just startled me a bit, is all."

"I didn't think gunfighters were so easy to startle."

"Looks like someone living here would get to know all about gunfighters."

"I've learned more about how stupid and arrogant men get when they get a gun in their hands," she said. "I've also learned just how bullheaded men can be when they get a little money in their pockets."

"You learn all that from changing sheets?" Clint asked with a grin.

For a moment, she glared angrily at him. Once she saw that Clint wasn't being serious, the dark-haired woman smacked him playfully on the shoulder. "Fine, then. You can change your own sheets."

Walking over to the bed, the woman set the pile of folded sheets down. Now that she was standing still, Clint was able to get a better look at her and he clearly liked what he saw.

She was of average height and slender build. She wasn't exactly skinny, but had more of a trim figure that only served to make her curves stand out more. Even though her dress was plainly cut, it would have taken a burlap sack to cover up the nice lines of her figure.

As she bent over to set down the sheets, Clint caught a good look at Claudia's tight backside. Rounded hips led up to a trim waist. When she turned around to place her hands upon those hips, Claudia stared at Clint with dark brown eyes. Clint was just quick enough to avoid admiring her perky breasts for longer than what was appropriate.

"How many men are working here?" Clint asked as he stepped in to close some of the distance between them.

"Enough to fill the bunkhouse," she replied. "At least, enough for me to stop cleaning up in there amid all the whistles and lewd comments."

"I'll try to keep those to a minimum."

Claudia wasn't quite quick enough to keep the smile from her face, so she turned on her heels and walked to another part of the room. "I suppose you'll be moving in there once Mr. Livingston makes his offer."

"You're a fortune teller as well? Impressive."

"I just saw your gun and figured you were here for the same reason as all them others."

"And what reason might that be?" Stopping before getting too close again, Clint took some of the joking tone from his voice. "I'd like to know what I might be in for instead of walking blindly into a hornet's nest."

Claudia looked him over a bit. She did a better job of hiding it this time, but she seemed to like what she saw as well. "All I know is that Mr. Livingston's been having words with Mr. Walsh, who shares a few property lines with him."

"There's been some shooting," Clint said. "I know that much."

"There sure has. Enough for both men to start hiring guns to work for them. I figured you were one of those."

"Not hardly."

Her eyes remained on Clint and took on an even more interested glint. "Then why are you here?"

Easing up to her, Clint got well within arm's reach without having Claudia run away. "One of Livingston's men has been shooting his mouth off claiming to be The Gunsmith."

She nodded. "I've heard as much. Tell you the truth, I'm not the only one who thinks he's full of hot air."

"He certainly is," Clint said. "You're a good judge of character."

With a subtle laugh under her breath, Claudia turned sharply and walked for the door. "I just happened to see that loudmouth in a saloon a few months back when he was answering to a name nobody heard of. Mr. Livingston just looks at most folks like they were part of the scenery unless they got something he wants. Sleep tight, now."

Clint smiled as he watched Claudia strut through his door and close it behind her.

SEVEN

Livingston stormed out of his house and stomped down the steps leading from his porch. His hands were clenched into fists and his mouth was set in a grim, straight line. Although a few people tried to acknowledge him as he passed them, they quickly stepped aside when they saw the no-nonsense look he wore.

Making a straight line from his home to one of the smaller buildings surrounding it, Livingston pushed open that door and stormed inside. That building resembled the upper floor of a hotel, since there was no front room or entryway to speak of. Instead, the door opened into a long hallway with several rooms facing each other down the row.

Some of the doors were open. Some were closed. Some were halfway in between. But Livingston wasn't interested in any of those. His eyes were firmly set upon a door at the end of the hall that was shut tight. When he reached it, Livingston took hold of the handle and tried to open the door. When he found it to be locked, the anger on his face deepened to a reddish hue.

"Open this door!" Livingston growled.

There wasn't so much as a peep from inside the room.

Pounding on the door, the Englishman said, "Open up, damn you, or I'll have it knocked down!"

From inside, a latch was pulled to one side and the door was eased open. The scarred face of the gunman looked through the crack as if he'd just heard a mildly funny joke. "That you out there, Emmett?"

Livingston tried to force open the door, but wasn't able to muscle it open. He was too angry to stop trying, however, and kept shoving at the stubborn slab of wood. When the gunman opened the door for him, Livingston stomped inside as if he'd kicked the door off its hinges.

"What's got you so worked up?" the gunman asked. "Did Walsh cut some more wire?"

After kicking the door shut, Livingston wheeled around to face the gunman with both hands propped upon his hips. "Who the hell are you?"

"Huh?"

"What's your name?"

"I told you, already. It's—"

"And before you say you're this Gunsmith person, I'll have you know that I am aware that is utterly false."

The gunman froze with the lie on the tip of his tongue. His mouth slowly closed as his eyes formed into slits. "You calling me a liar?"

Livingston took his hands from his hips and backed off a step until he almost knocked over a small table. "Y-you heard me. I said that I don't think you're The Gunsmith."

"And why not?"

"Because a man's brought it to my attention that he is the true Gunsmith."

"And you believed him just because he said so?"

Straightening up a bit, Livingston shot back with, "I made that same mistake when I believed you."

The gunman stared Livingston down for a good couple of seconds. Each of those seconds ticked by like they were marking off the final moments of someone's life. In that time, the gunman mulled over what he'd heard, until he finally allowed the mean glare to fade from his eyes.

"So what?" the gunman grunted. "You want us to prove which is which? You want to have us fight it out for you to settle who's who?"

"No! With everything that's going on, I just want to know who I'm dealing with. I don't even know who this Gunsmith person is, so I don't know where to begin in making anyone prove they're him. I've heard the name mentioned here and there, but that's about it.

"From what I've seen and heard, I don't want the sort of man who'd claim to be him poking their nose into my affairs. All this other fellow wants is to set the record straight."

"You sure about that?"

"Yes."

There were another few silent moments during which Livingston did his best to stare down the gunman. The gunman, on the other hand, seemed to just be biding his time.

"All right," the gunman said. "I'm not The Gunsmith. My name's not Clint Adams, but that don't mean whoever you were talking to is that man either."

"Frankly, I don't care about that. You're doing the job I hired you for just fine."

Slowly, the gunman started to nod. "Okay, then. Are we done?"

"Not quite. I still would like to know your name."

"You can call me Wade."

"Is that it? Is that short for anything?"

"That's my name and I'll answer to it. That's all you need to know."

"Will I get someone coming around complaining about that in a while?"

Wade didn't reply with words, so much as he did with an intent scowl.

"Fine, fine," Livingston said. "Wade it is. Have you made any progress on that other matter we were discussing?"

"Oh, you mean those other men I recommended?"

Glancing around nervously, the Englishman nodded. "That's it."

"I've put a list together, but it would help if we knew a bit more about what we were up against. I'm thinking we might be able to buy one of Walsh's men."

"Buy one of his men?"

"Buy, bribe, pay off, whatever you like. Throw enough money out there and one of those men will surely bite. That way we can have some inside knowledge. A little of that will go a long ways in putting an end to this thing."

Livingston nodded. "Good idea. I think I'll set aside some funds for that very thing."

"Good. While you're at it, there's one more thing. I'd like to meet this new guest of yours."

EIGHT

After Claudia left, Clint seemed to have been forgotten inside that big house. He didn't plan on staying long, so he didn't bother unpacking anything from his saddlebags. That left him with plenty of time on his hands, which he used to explore as much of the house as he could.

Clint wandered throughout the mansion, poking his nose in where he could. For the most part, everyone there was very accommodating. Since he didn't force open any locked doors or do anything to make an ass of himself, he was greeted with friendly nods or the occasional wave.

The house was like an old museum; fancy but stuffy. Although lots of it was impressive, Clint found himself wanting to get out before too long. All he had to do was follow his nose, and he soon made his way to one of the side exits that opened onto the rest of the property.

As far as he could tell, the spread was some sort of ranch. There were a few barns and the stables, along with some long bunkhouses. Still, the place didn't seem busy enough to be a ranch. The sun might have been dipping beneath the horizon, but any ranch would have been hectic compared to the stillness that surrounded Livingston's place.

Clint made his way to one of the bunkhouses and saw plenty of men walking in and out on their way to one of the smaller buildings nearby. There were plenty of lights inside the place and several shadows moving behind the covered windows. But despite all those workers, not one of them was doing any chores outside.

It seemed that most of the manual labor was done by a few workers who'd crossed Clint's path several times in the short duration he'd been there. The longer Clint stood and watched what little activity there was around him, the more convinced he was that he'd be leaving the next morning.

That should give him plenty of time to make sure his message had been received. Clint also was fairly certain he'd cross paths with whoever had been impersonating him. Any man that wanted to use his name would be anxious to meet the genuine article.

Of course, it was hard to say if the man would shake Clint's hand or try to take a shot at him. Either way, it should be over soon enough.

When Clint heard the shot crack through the air to his right, he wondered if he'd fatally underestimated his imposter. He shifted on the balls of his feet while dropping into a crouch. By the time he was facing in the direction of the gunshot, his hand was on the grip of the modified Colt and ready to draw the weapon.

Either nobody noticed him standing there, or they were too busy trying to figure out what they were going to do about what they'd heard. Before anyone could take notice of Clint, one of the young men working the land came running toward the nearby bunkhouse.

"Some of Walsh's boys are riding up to the house! One of them took a shot at us!"

Although that wasn't good news, it was something to light a similar fire under all the hired hands. No longer chattering to each other or deciding what to do, every last one of them wrapped their hands around a firearm and headed in the direction where the worker was pointing.

Clint decided to tag along at the back of the group so he could get a look at what was happening. He kept his Colt in its holster for the time being, but was still ready to draw in a heartbeat if things took a turn for the worse.

He didn't have to follow the other men very far before another series of shots hissed through the air. Reflexively, Clint ducked down and looked for some cover. Since the shots were all coming from the same direction, he got himself against the closest building and pressed his back against it so there was at least one wall between himself and the incoming lead.

The rest of the men were either too eager or too inexperienced to make the same move before taking quick aim and pulling their triggers.

Peeking around the corner, Clint was able to pick out four shapes rushing toward the group that had emerged from the bunkhouse. Those shapes were easy enough to pick out since they were carrying torches in one hand and blazing away with pistols in the other.

A few of the men from the bunkhouse had stepped out a bit further than the rest. They'd dropped to one knee and were returning fire. As the riders drew closer, the fire between them and Livingston's men got worse. In those brief pops of light, Clint was able to see another group of men that he'd missed before.

Although these men were heading for the bunkhouse, they weren't on horseback. They weren't even firing their guns, despite the fact that they each had rifles in their hands. In fact, as far as Clint could see, these men running toward the bunkhouse might have been smiling.

"It's a raiding party!" one of the men at the bunkhouse shouted. "Gun 'em all down before they kill someone!"

More fire erupted from more barrels than Clint could

count. It was like standing in the middle of a raging thunderstorm, with sound and fury coming in from all sides.

The riders had peeled off in opposite directions rather than continue their charge toward the bunkhouse. One of the men seemed to be slouched in his saddle and might have been hit. Only one of the men near the bunkhouse was on the ground, and that one was still moving and trying to take aim again.

Only when he saw the riders turn tail and head away from the bunkhouse did Clint step out from his cover and make his presence known.

"They're running off!" Clint shouted over the continuing gunfire coming from the men around the bunkhouse. "They're not even firing anymore!"

But the men weren't listening to a word Clint was saying. On the contrary, some of them were planting their feet and taking more careful aim at the backs of the retreating riders.

Clint ran forward until he was close enough to reach one of the men taking aim. "Goddammit, hold your fire!" he snarled while forcing the man's gun toward the sky.

The pistol went off and sent its round into the clouds. The man who'd fired it turned around to fix savage eyes upon Clint. "What the hell do you think you're doing?"

"You ran them off. There's no need to shoot them in the back."

"Who the hell are you?"

A few guns were still going off, but the crackle was dying out quickly. From the corners of his eyes, Clint could see more and more of the men closing in around him.

Clint took half a step back just to show that he wasn't going to pose a threat. To that effect, he even dropped his Colt back into its holster. "It's all over. They're gone."

"Yeah. No thanks to you."

"What's going on here?" one of the other men asked.

The man closest to Clint said, "This one here kept me from dropping one of them assholes."

"There were plenty others trying to put bullets in their backs," Clint said calmly. "No need for one more."

"You calling us cowards?"

"I can tell you what I saw, and that was a bunch of men running away with twice as many men trying to take advantage of that. You can call it whatever you like."

Another man walked toward Clint. Unlike the rest, his eyes were cold and calm. His scarred face barely registered any emotion until he was close enough to get a good look at Clint.

"I never seen you around here," Wade said. "Are you Livingston's guest?"

Clint nodded.

"Then I think I've got a matter to settle with you."

NINE

There was still some commotion following the shots that had been fired, but everyone seemed to be recovering from that fairly quickly. Already, a few men had jumped onto horses and taken off after the riders, and the rest were already going about their business. Wade and Clint, on the other hand, stayed right where they were.

"So, you're the one claiming to be The Gunsmith?" Wade asked.

Without missing a beat, Clint replied, "You took the words right out of my mouth."

"Fair enough. Care for a drink?"

Clint had been expecting plenty of different things, but this wasn't one of them. "Sure," he replied warily.

Turning his back on Clint and walking to one of the smaller buildings, Wade motioned for Clint to follow him. Soon, both men were standing in front of a building that was larger than a shack, but smaller than a cabin. It was narrow and had a large opening along one wall. The smells drifting from inside that building told Clint right away that it was the local equivalent of a chuck wagon.

Wade knocked on a small ledge at the bottom of the

opening in the side of the wall. When a fat man wearing a dirty shirt appeared, Wade said, "Two beers."

"This ain't a saloon," the fat man replied.

"Yeah, any saloon would have better service. Come on, now, I know you got some beer in there. Pour us two." With an overexaggerated Southern accent, he added, "All that shooting plumb shook us up."

The fat man smirked and shook his head. He also poured two dented mugs full with a frothy brew.

"Thanks," Wade said.

The fat man already had his back turned and tossed half a wave toward the window. After that, he was gone.

"It's warm as piss," Wade cautioned, "but it gets the job done."

Clint took a sip and winced. The second sip, however, wasn't too bad. "Appreciate the beer," Clint said. "Now how about you tell me what the hell is going on around here."

Having walked to a hitching post that was being used at the moment, Wade leaned against it and took another sip of beer. Gazing up at the dark sky, he said, "You already met Livingston?"

"Yeah."

"What about a man by the name of Martin Walsh?"

Clint shook his head.

"Walsh is about as rich as Livingston, only he made his money as a rancher."

"What about Livingston? All I could gather is that he's rich."

"Then you're right there with the rest of us. Near as I could figure, he's a land baron. I've heard him mention some mines in the area, but I don't think he's made much off of them.

"Anyways, Livingston and Walsh fight like cats and dogs. They're neighbors, so they're always arguing about this fence being two feet on the wrong side or that animal straying three steps in the wrong direction. Bunch of goddamn whining if you ask me."

"I haven't met one rich man yet who just sits back and enjoys what he's got," Clint said.

Wade lifted his mug. "I'll drink to that."

"So when did they start hiring gunhands?" Clint asked. "And why was Livingston told that one of those gunhands was me?"

Nodding slowly, Wade cringed as though he'd assumed that particular bullet had already been dodged. "You've got my apologies on that one, Adams. I hope it didn't cause any trouble."

"Trouble? You've only been killing men and claiming to be me. What trouble could that possibly cause?"

"You gotta believe me, Adams. I didn't think it would go that far. I only passed myself off as you to get the job. Hell, I figured I'd just need to show my gun to scare away a couple loudmouthed cowboys."

"Livingston acted like he barely even knew who I was," Clint said. "I doubt you had to do anything so drastic to impress him."

"And if I would'a known that then, I wouldn't have mentioned your name at all."

"Is that something you do a lot?"

"Nah. I was just hearing about you being in these parts a few days before Livingston started asking around for help. He was paying good money for experienced men and there were plenty of takers wanting to beat me out of a job. I said I was you to get one of those spots."

"Does anyone else around here think you're me?" Clint asked.

After a slight pause, Wade said, "These men don't know any better."

"That's just great."

"I already set it straight with Livingston. If the subject

comes up again with anyone else, I'll set them straight, too. How's that?"

Clint studied the man's face carefully. Although his instincts told him not to believe what he said, his eyes told him that Wade was telling the truth. "If I find out you're blowing smoke—"

"I'm not," Wade assured him. "The reason I dropped your name was because you've got one hell of a reputation with a shooting iron. You're the last man I'd want to cross."

"If I find out you're lying, I'll make you sorry you even heard of me."

"I wouldn't expect anything less."

"All right, then."

"If you want to make some good money, I'd consider staying on."

"I think I've had my fill of this place."

Wade shrugged. "Livingston pays well and he pays in cash."

"Why pay so well for hired guns?"

"Because of that thing I was telling you about concerning Martin Walsh. I don't know who started hiring on the guns first, but there's been shots fired back and forth for a few months now. Before tonight, there was a section of fence that was cut and some cows wandered across. Both rich men came face-to-face over that one and neither one had the guts to say they had anything to do with it."

"Did it result in any shooting?" Clint asked.

"Hell, yes. One man on each side was killed."

"From what I hear, there's been a few other men killed."

Wade only had to see the fire in Clint's eyes to know which men he was talking about. "When I was first hired on, there was a big chunk of land that Walsh carved off for his own. It took a hell of a fight to get it back. Livingston lost a few of his own men, too, so don't think I was the only one pulling a trigger."

"Maybe not, but your trigger was the one that nearly landed me in jail."

"Again, I'm sorry about that. Won't happen again."

"Hasn't the law been coming around to look in on all this shooting?"

Wade let out a chuckle when he heard that. "The closest law is in Paso Negro and they draw their salaries from these rich folks out here. Them or the politicians may not be outright crooked, but they owe Livingston and Walsh a whole string of favors. Besides, all that's happened has been out here in the middle of nowhere. Plenty of men are killed and buried without the rest of the world knowing about it."

"Unless they were killed by The Gunsmith."

Wade lowered his head and winced. "I wish I could fix that, but—"

Patting Wade on the shoulder, Clint said, "Oh, you're going to help fix it. I've got a few ideas on how you can do that very thing."

TEN

If Clint needed any more proof that the shootings were a common occurrence, he got it when dinner was served only slightly later than usual. The cook apologized for making him wait and then handed over a plate of beef stew and bread. Since nobody else seemed too shaken about what had happened, Clint enjoyed his meal and went back to his room.

It was past ten o'clock at night when he heard a knock on his door. "Yeah?" he grunted.

"It's Claudia."

Clint glanced over to the door, thinking back to the last time he'd seen the black-haired woman. As far as he could remember, that was her voice. "Come in."

The door came open just enough for Claudia to poke her head in and say, "I know it's late. Are you decent?"

"Not even close."

As he figured, that didn't keep her from looking in his direction. She made a show out of looking disappointed. "You're dressed."

"Yes, I am. I'm not quite decent, though. At least, not in every sense of the word."

She brushed away the joke, stepped into the room, and

41

closed the door behind her. "I thought I'd fix up your bed for you."

Clint glanced over to the pile of sheets, which were still neatly folded and sitting right where she'd left them the last time she'd been in the room. "You just figured I'd be the sort of man to leave that until the last minute?"

Claudia walked over to the sheets and started tucking them into place. "You're a man. It's a safe bet you'll leave most everything until the last minute."

"Sounds like you've got some experience in that area."

"I clean up after plenty of them. I should know what I'm talking about. What's that you're doing?"

Following her eyes, Clint looked down to the saddle-bags hung over the chair in front of him. "Just making sure everything's where it should be."

"That's funny. Most folks that visit here aren't worried about getting their things stolen from their room. Come to think of it, I'm a bit offended by that."

"Don't be. I'm doing this because I'm heading out of here in the morning."

This time, the disappointment on her face wasn't a joke. "You're leaving? So soon? Why?"

"There's some things I need to check on."

Claudia finished up the corner she was working on and walked over to where Clint was standing. She wore a dress that wasn't exactly fancy, but wasn't as plain as the one she'd had on earlier. It was made from dark gray material and hugged her body nicely. The bodice was laced up tightly to show her narrow waist and rounded hips. It also made her pert breasts stand out proudly, with just a hint of cleavage on display.

"Don't let all that shooting scare you off," she said. "It happens all the time."

"You say that like it's a good thing."

She shook her head and reached out to run her hands along the sides of his arms. "It's just men with guns trying to scare each other. It's sort of like drunks screaming at each other in a saloon. It's not good, but it just . . . happens."

Nodding, Clint placed his hands upon her shoulders and looked straight into her eyes. "Men have been killed already. Doesn't that bother you?"

"Of course it does."

"And more will get killed unless something changes."

Claudia's eyes narrowed a bit and her voiced dropped to a serious pitch. "The world won't exactly miss men like these. Having them shoot at each other may just clean out some of the trash around here."

"If it's so bad, why not pack up and leave?"

She shrugged. "Because nobody's shot at any of the wrong people. Not yet, anyway."

"Kind of makes me wonder why I want to see this through and I just got here."

Placing her hands upon Clint's chest, Claudia said, "I was wondering why you'd want to leave, myself. Especially when I had so many good plans for you."

"Really? Do they involve straightening up those sheets some more?"

"Actually, I was thinking more along the lines of messing them up."

ELEVEN

Claudia pressed herself up against Clint and stood on her tiptoes so she could place her lips directly upon his. Her skin was smooth as silk and warm to the touch. The moment Clint responded to her kiss, she opened her mouth and let the tip of her tongue flick across his lips.

Clint's hands went straight to her hips, holding her close while feeling her shift back and forth. As she continued to lick his lips, Claudia let out a sound that sounded a lot like a satisfied purr. Soon, her fingers were sliding through Clint's hair and tickling the back of his ear.

"Is this the kind of service all of Mr. Livingston's guests get?" Clint asked.

Smiling, Claudia replied, "You keep joking like that and you might just wind up with crisp sheets after all."

"Well, now," Clint said as he tightened his grip around Claudia's waist, "we can't have that." As he spoke, Clint lifted Claudia off her feet and spun her around until her legs brushed against the bed.

She let out a surprised yelp, while quickly accommodating him as he lowered her down and crawled on top of her. "And here I was starting to think you weren't interested."

Clint didn't even bother responding to that. Instead, he

44

took hold of her hands and pinned them to the bed. From there, he started kissing her gently along the side of her neck, and made his way all the way down to the spot where her breasts swelled against the restraints of her dress.

Claudia lay back and savored every one of the kisses placed against her skin. Even when Clint was no longer pinning her hands to the mattress, she kept her arms stretched up over her head so she could arch her back luxuriously.

Running the tips of his fingers along the laces that kept her dress tied shut, Clint said, "You know what I like most about these things?"

"What?"

"This one string, right here." As he said that, he found the loose string and pulled on it until the entire side of her dress began to unravel. Since Claudia was laughing at the way he went about undressing her, it made Clint's job that much easier.

After a bit of wriggling and a small amount of struggle, she emerged from her bodice and let out a relieved sigh. The skirt wasn't such a chore to remove, but Clint took his time in running his hands up underneath the material so he could slide them along the smooth legs he found there.

Claudia's hands rubbed Clint's shoulders, urging him on and subtly moving him to where she wanted him to go. As Clint eased her skirts up, she slowly spread her legs for him, and let out another contented sigh when she felt Clint's hands move up along her inner thigh.

When Clint saw the smooth, creamy skin of her legs, it was plain instinct that made him kiss his way up toward her knees. Her skin was so soft against his mouth and tasted so good that he kept right on kissing her until her skirts were bunched up around her waist and she was lifting her hips to meet his mouth.

"Oh, my God," she whispered when she felt Clint pull off her underwear and touch the silky lips of her pussy. When she felt his tongue slide along those same lips and trace a quick line to her clitoris, she didn't have enough breath to say much of anything.

Claudia grabbed the back of Clint's head and held him in place so he wouldn't stop what he was doing. Every flick of his tongue sent shivers through her body. Even the feel of his breath against her delicate skin was enough to bring her close to an orgasm.

When he could feel her body start to tremble even harder, Clint moved his mouth up higher to trace a line along her flat stomach. He let his mouth wander between her breasts and all the way up to her neck. By that time, he'd shrugged out of his pants and kicked them to the floor. Clint settled between her legs and felt his hard penis rubbing against her slick pussy.

Reaching down to guide him into her, Claudia wrapped her legs around him and let out a trembling sigh when she felt him ease all the way inside. After Clint had pumped in and out of her a few times, the orgasm that had teased her before was coming back in force.

Claudia's arms tightened around him and her breath started coming in quick gasps. The muscles of her thighs turned into strips of steel and her hips began to buck against him. All of that prompted Clint to quicken his own pace and he watched as Claudia arched her back and let the climax roll through her.

For a moment, she held her breath.

When she let it out again, a wide smile filled her face and her muscles finally relaxed.

"Good Lord," she breathed. "I've been thinking about that since the first time I came in here."

"You know what I've been thinking about?" Clint asked.

"What?"

Rather than say another word, Clint let his actions speak for him as he raised up so he was kneeling between Claudia's legs. He was still inside her, so he reached down to cup her tight buttocks in his hands and lifted her off the bed so he could impale her once more.

Her eyes widened a bit in surprise, which quickly turned into sheer pleasure. Reaching out to grip onto the bed with both hands, she wriggled and bucked in his hands in time to Clint's rhythm. Soon, their bodies were moving perfectly together as he pumped in and out of her again and again.

Clint leaned forward a bit so he could reach down and cup one of her breasts in his hand. Supporting her with his other hand, he slowed his pace down a bit so he could savor the feel of her naked skin against his hand.

Although Claudia tried to get out of the rest of her clothes, she was unable to shake free of everything without stopping altogether. Since that was out of the question, she propped herself up on her elbows and began pumping her hips in earnest.

The sight of Claudia's disheveled clothes, tussled hair, and hungry eyes was enough to get Clint's heart beating even faster. Her skirts were bunched up just enough for him to get between her legs, and her clothes were pulled open just enough for him to put his hands upon her where he pleased.

The only thing either of them cared about was pleasing each other. Nothing else mattered. Once both of them realized that, the intensity of their lovemaking flared like a fire that had just been fed some extra fuel. In fact, she started playing up to it by pulling her clothes open for him now and then before covering herself just to tease him.

With a mischievous smile on her face, she pushed Clint back while scooting away from him on the bed. She got onto her knees and ran her fingertips along the soft skin between her breasts while licking her lips. Smiling at the reaction that got from him, Claudia turned around to grab the headboard and glance back at Clint over her shoulder.

Seeing that little grin and the glint in Claudia's eyes was more than enough for Clint to get the hint. He moved up behind her, lifted the back of her skirt, and slid the palm of his hand along the curve of her hip. A few seconds later, his cock was sliding into her from behind and Clint was thrusting back and forth.

Claudia hung onto the headboard and arched her back as Clint grabbed onto her hips and drove deeply into her. Soon, another climax was taking her breath away. Clint only had to pump a few more times before he was right there with her.

TWELVE

It was just shy of noon on the next day when things were stirring up again at the line dividing Livingston's and Walsh's property. After all that had gone on before, armed riders were now patrolling the area to keep watch on anything bigger than a rabbit trying to cross from one side of the fence to the other.

Walsh's men appeared to be more anxious than Livingston's to patrol the outer stretches of land. Clint picked up on that much when he gave himself a tour of Livingston's land after breakfast. It was an impressive amount of property, but he was surprised that most of the hired guns seemed to be sticking to the middle of it. Walsh, on the other hand, seemed to be taking a more direct approach.

Clint had barely crossed the property line before he spotted a couple of riders from Walsh's side headed in his direction. Considering all the tension between the two factions, Clint brought Eclipse to a stop and calmly waited for the riders to approach. They got to him in a rush and glared at him over the barrels of their rifles.

"Who the hell are you?" the first man asked.

"I'd like to have a word with Mr. Walsh," Clint replied. "Could you take me to him?"

"What's this concerning?"

"If it's all the same to you, I'd rather just explain it once to him."

"You'd best explain it to me, or you won't get to set eyes on Mr. Walsh." The rider's eyes narrowed as he raised his rifle a bit when he added, "In fact, you may not even draw another breath unless you explain yourself here and now."

"I've been over at Mr. Livingston's place."

"Yeah, I can see that."

Ignoring the interruption, Clint continued. "I had a word with him about the matter between him and your boss. I'd just like to hear both sides before passing any judgments."

"And who the hell are you? Why should anyone care what you think about anything?"

"My name's Clint Adams. I've dealt with things like this before and might just be of some assistance."

Both of the riders recognized Clint's name. That much was clear by the way they glanced nervously back and forth at each other. In fact, both of them lowered their rifles just enough to show they weren't about to fire quite yet.

"You're Clint Adams?" the second man asked.

"I am."

"We heard you were working for Mr. Livingston."

"Yeah," the first one grunted. "We also heard you been working for him long enough to have killed a few of our boys."

"Don't believe everything you hear," Clint said, fighting the urge to set the record straight right then and there. "Besides, if I was so intent on killing Walsh's men, wouldn't I have tried something with you two by now?"

Going by the looks on the two riders' faces, they either believed Clint outright or didn't want to push him into going for his gun. Either way, they lowered their rifles and motioned for Clint to follow them.

"Come on," the first rider said. "We'll take you along to see if Mr. Walsh wants to speak to you."

Clint knew well enough what both of the other men were thinking. If Walsh didn't want to speak to Clint, there would be plenty of other men to back up the first two and help them take Clint down for good. While Clint wasn't too pleased with the idea of strolling into a hostile camp, he figured his odds were pretty good in being able to get out of there if he wanted to.

He'd seen Walsh's men fight. If those raiders from the night before were any indication, Clint should be able to walk in and out of Walsh's home however many times he pleased without being in too much danger.

Then again, there was always the possibility that those raiders were just the most anxious of Walsh's men instead of the most skilled with a firearm. Rather than work himself into a lather trying to sort through all the possibilities, Clint went along for the ride and followed his two guides straight into the heart of Walsh's property.

He would just have to find out the hard way whether or not he would be able to get out again.

THIRTEEN

Clint heard every one of Martin Walsh's steps as they knocked against the floor. The house was more of what one might expect at the middle of a sprawling ranch. It was flat and angular, like a piece of brick-shaped clay that had been dropped onto a rock floor. Even the furnishings, as Clint would discover, were straight ahead and to the point.

Martin Walsh, himself, belonged in that house in every respect. Like the building around him, he was stocky and angular. His features were straight lines cut into wet stucco. Although he moved like a man in his late thirties, the scowl on his face would have been much more comfortable upon a grizzled, battle-hardened old Army officer.

"Who's this?" Walsh grunted as he stood in the doorway. "If he wants a job, have him check in with Pardee."

"You should talk to this one yourself, Mr. Walsh," the first rider said. "We found him out by the fence. He says he's Clint Adams."

"The Gunsmith?" Walsh asked as he took another, more careful look at Clint.

Nodding, Clint said, "I've been called that as well as plenty of other things."

"How about murderer?" Walsh shot back. "It been a while since someone called you that?"

All the men in the vicinity stopped what they were doing and focused their eyes on Clint. More than a few hands wandered closer to holstered guns. One or two guns might have even snuck out into overly anxious hands.

Although he could feel the tension in the air, Clint didn't respond to it. He kept his face neutral and his body completely still. "Yeah," he replied honestly. "Some folks have called me that."

Walsh was a few inches shorter than Clint. Even so, he didn't seem to look up as he glared into Clint's eyes. He carried himself like he was perched on top of a mountain, taking in everything around him. When he stared at Clint, he nodded slowly and said, "You don't say that with much pride."

"That's not the sort of thing to be proud of, sir."

"Is it true?"

"I've killed men," Clint said. "But only when there wasn't any choice. Far too many of them were after me just for bragging rights. The way I see it, they signed their own death warrant."

Walsh began to nod. "The rest of you men can go. Let me and Mr. Adams here have a talk."

A few of the men lingered so they could get a better look at Walsh's face. When they saw the certainty in Walsh's eyes coupled with the quick way in which he shooed them off, the last of the stragglers found something else to occupy their time.

"All right, then," Walsh said. "You came all this way to talk, so talk."

"Frankly, I'm surprised I was able to see you so easily."

"I've met plenty of men in my day, Adams. Lately, I've had to deal with plenty of undesirable characters, but you don't strike me as one of them. I will have you know that if

you twitch toward that gun of yours, you'll have a hell of a
time getting out of this house alive."

"I don't doubt that. You've got some good men." Although he meant those words, Clint refrained from men-
tioning the riders he was able to avoid while he'd been
looking for a good spot to cross over the fence.

"Somehow, I doubt you wanted to compliment my
men."

"No. Actually, I wanted to ask you about what's going
on between you and Mr. Livingston."

"You were working for him. Don't you already know?"

"I heard his side of it and it was little more than a few
sketchy details. I thought you might be able to fill in some
of the missing pieces."

Walsh led Clint through the house. He walked with
solid, confident steps and kept his hands clasped behind his
back. When he went into a large office with a large desk set
up in front of a large window, he stopped. Amazingly
enough, the stout man didn't appear to be dwarfed by his
own surroundings. On the contrary, he filled up as much
space as his body would allow.

The only thing that could be considered decoration in
the office was a map hanging on one of the walls adjacent
to the window. Even that obviously had its practical use,
with markings indicating several property lines and other
points of interest on either side of the fence.

Reaching out to grab a cigar from a polished box, Walsh
asked, "What's your interest in all this?"

"There's a lot of shooting going on and there's got to be
something behind it."

Walsh was shaking his head as he lit his cigar. "There's
plenty of hired guns to go around and not one of them
gives much of a damn as to why the shots are being fired.
All they ask is who they should aim at."

"I'm not just some hired gun."

"Ah, yes. You're the infamous Gunsmith. That explains

everything." The sarcasm in Walsh's voice wasn't hard to miss.

The longer he talked to Walsh, the more Clint changed his opinion of the man. Granted, his original opinion was skewed by what Livingston and his men had said, but Walsh was a lot sharper than Clint would have expected. He could see an intelligence in the man's eyes that would have been a true threat at a poker table.

"Let's put it this way," Clint said. "I've seen plenty of men shooting at each other. I've seen battlefields and I've seen street fights. What I've seen around here has been nothing short of chaos.

"Riders come screaming in, firing their guns, and are chased off in a matter of minutes. Gunmen are hired, only to be stored up like hay in a barn. It might just be a disorganized feud, but there are men getting killed and plenty more blood to be spilled. Something's not right. I can smell it."

"Oh, you can smell it?" Walsh grunted.

"Yes, I can. As near as I could tell, Livingston doesn't have much livestock and isn't even set up to handle more than he's got. His land might have some potential, but that only makes it all the more confusing why you would send men to shoot up his house rather than try to take a real stab at him.

"I've only ridden once across your property, but that was enough to see the cattle you've got. With all the grazing land I saw as well as all the feed you've got stored up, I'm guessing you've got plenty more cattle on their way to or from a major drive."

"Try three drives," Walsh corrected as he offered Clint a cigar.

Clint took the cigar as well as the match that came along with it. He wasn't normally one for smoking, but having the cigar in Walsh's office seemed as natural as having a drink in a saloon. "Obviously, you see my point. Despite the fact that you share a fence line, you and Livingston don't seem to have much of a reason to fight. And even if you do, you two haven't seemed to be putting your hearts into it. I'm not proposing a war, but it seems odd that one hasn't broken out just yet. With all these guns, all these men, all this bad blood between you, there's got to be some reason why things haven't boiled over."

Walsh's lips curled into a smile around the cigar in his mouth. He'd listened carefully to every last word Clint had said, even nodding here and there as Clint made his points. "You seem to have a pretty good nose, Mr. Adams."

"It's served me well so far."

"Since you managed to sniff out all the bad blood between me and Livingston, I'm surprised you couldn't figure out the rest."

"Enlighten me."

"There's plenty of blood between me and that Englishman," Walsh stated as he puffed his cigar. "We're brothers."

FOURTEEN

Clint nodded as various pieces of the puzzle fit together in his head. Even though the relationship between Walsh and Livingston wasn't expected, it was the sort of surprise that felt like finally being able to pull off his boot and scratch the spot on the bottom of his foot that had been driving him crazy for hours.

"Brothers, huh?" Clint said.

"Yep. Unfortunately, that's how it's been our whole lives."

"That explains the halfhearted attempts on each other's lives."

Walsh let out half a laugh and rolled his cigar between thumb and forefinger. "Like plenty of brothers, we've been nipping at each other since we were pups. Things got really bad after our father passed on."

"Was he the one that brought you two to this country?" When Clint saw the flicker of surprise on Walsh's face, he explained, "I've heard you two called the Englishman and Irishman more than once. Judging by Livingston's spread, I'd say he at least spent some time across the ocean. Since you two don't look too far apart in age, I guessed that meant you spent some time there as well."

"You got a sharp set of eyes, Adams. That's partly how I figured you to be the real Gunsmith instead of that other fellow working for Livingston."

"That's a matter I hope is resolved."

Walsh laughed again. "I said those very same words when dealing with my brother. Unfortunately, things don't work out that way."

"Since you two have taken on different names and are sending raiding parties to each other's homes, I'd wager you don't get along too well."

"Another good observation, Adams. You might say that started back when me and Emmett were growing up. Our father did a lot of traveling and set up homes in England as well as Ireland. There's probably more, but he managed to keep those a better secret than the other two.

"I found out I had a brother when I was nine years old. We would visit now and then, but it took a toll on our mothers and eventually caused them both to tell our father to go to hell." After pulling in a smoky breath, Walsh let it out by saying, "He went to America instead and took us along for the ride."

"Sounds rough."

"It was, but it was also an adventure. Don't get me wrong. My father was a good enough man. He had an eye for the ladies, but that's not the worst sin a man can have. Wouldn't you agree?"

Clint had to grin and shake his head. "It's one that can get you into plenty of trouble."

"Yes, indeed. But my father gave us a choice in staying with our mothers or going with him to this country. Me and my brother both chose to come here, but even then we were fighting so much that we wanted to keep our mothers' last names. Looking back on it, I think we both did that just to get under each other's skin.

"Apart from a rocky start, we had a good life here. Still, me and my brother never passed up a chance to make each other's life hell. We grew into two very different men and when my father passed on, we thought we wouldn't bother keeping in touch.

"But my father was smarter than the both of us," Walsh continued. "He must have known what would happen, so he left us both the same amount of land. Actually, he cut one chunk of property into two pieces and left one to each of us. There's good land for cattle and even some mineral veins running through this land. I suppose it was my father's plan to see to it me and Emmett stayed close so we could keep up our financial situation."

"But that's not how things worked out," Clint said.

"No, it sure wasn't. Both the cattle and mining businesses are ebb-and-flow kinds of affairs. Sometimes, they're booming and other times they're busted. Since they don't ebb and flow along the same schedules, we both saw each other as having the better end of the stick at different times. Needless to say, that sparked a bit of . . . brotherly animosity."

"Is that your father's term for it?" Clint asked.

"My mother's. More than once, believe me, I wished I was back in Ireland with her and our dozen head of sheep. Things were a whole lot simpler back then."

"Before you and your brother started shooting at each other?"

Just hearing that was like a cloud passing over Walsh's face. He lowered his eyes, considered it for a moment, and finally nodded. "You might say that was my fault. Not quite ten years ago, Emmett found a nice strike of silver in one of the mines on his property."

"Mines?"

"Yeah. There's a few here and there on his land as well as a few that are in his name nearby. Anyway, I was struggling through an epidemic that wiped out almost half my herd and was desperate for some money. Since I wasn't so willing to lend a hand the year before when Emmett was getting by on finding a few gold flakes a month, he thought he'd return the favor.

"I called him out and said we should just put an end to our fighting once and for all. Since neither was gonna share, we should just put everything on the table and see who walks away with it." Wincing, Walsh added, "I was drunk. That's probably why I missed."

"You wouldn't be the first man to take a shot at his brother," Clint pointed out. "Usually, there's a better reason why so many of them miss."

"Whatever reason I had doesn't much matter. He came after me and I came after him. This is all over the course of years, you understand. Finally, we both get our businesses running just so we can afford to hire men to do our fighting for us. Now, it's too late to look back."

"I can't believe that. You are brothers, after all. Neither one of you would truly kill one another, would you?"

"I wouldn't be so sure about that."

"Why?"

"Because that English prick might be the reason my father's not drawing breath anymore."

Clint was more surprised at the calm way Walsh said that last part than he was at the words themselves. Still, despite the unwavering coolness in Walsh's voice, there was no denying the power of his statement.

"Whatever happened," Clint said, "shooting at each other won't help you resolve it."

"It might or it might not. All I know is that I can't just sit back and let Emmett keep whittling away at what's mine. If I do that, there won't be anything left. In the end, that's probably what he's after."

"Maybe all you two need is someone in the middle to help tie up these loose ends."

"A mediator, huh?" Walsh said with a snorting laugh. "I suppose that person should be someone like yourself?"

"Seeing as how such a mediator would need to get in the

middle of two bunches of hired guns, I'd say I'm qualified for the position."

"And I doubt there'd be anyone else foolish enough to take the job."

"There's that, too."

"How about I think it over?" Walsh offered. "In the meantime, you can stay here as my guest."

"Oh, that won't be necessary," Clint said. As the words were coming out of his mouth, he spotted the armed men blocking the doorway.

"Please," Walsh said. "I insist."

FIFTEEN

The men in the doorway to the office didn't look particularly threatening. In fact, they looked like they were about to apologize for getting in Clint's way if he wanted to leave. The fact that they were there at all was more of a statement from Walsh than anything else.

Like the way he dealt with his brother, Walsh was getting his point across just hard enough for it to be taken seriously. As it turned out, the men standing there weren't even told to go for their guns. They didn't have to, since Clint accepted the offer to stay on at Walsh's ranch so the owner could consider his offer.

Clint was escorted from the office to the back of the house. Along the way, he passed by many of the rooms and was able to get a fairly good look at most of the house. It was a comfortable spread, and was even bigger than Clint had thought from seeing it from the front. Even though it was a bit smaller than Livingston's house, it seemed a whole lot emptier.

Another big difference between this house and Livingston's was the fact that Clint was shown straight through the house and out the back door. There appeared to be more than a few empty bedrooms in the house, but they were all behind Clint now. In front of him were a couple narrow structures resembling the bunkhouses on the Englishman's property.

Those bunkhouses, like Livingston's appeared to be full of hired hands, all of whom wore guns strapped around their waists. Those men gave Clint an appraising eye as he was brought to them and shown into the second of three narrow buildings.

Clint hadn't seen too much of Livingston's bunkhouses, but they couldn't have been as nice as the ones Walsh had. The bunkhouse Clint was taken to resembled a fairly nice hotel. There was a small dining room in the front and two short hallways with doors facing each other on either side. The air smelled like baking bread, which must have also caught the attention of Clint's guide.

"Lunch'll be served in a bit," the man said. "Supper's at six-thirty. You want anything else in the meantime, you can take it up with the cook."

"How about if I want to leave?" Clint asked as a way to test the waters. "Who should I see about that?"

"You can do what you want," the man said with a shrug. "But if Mr. Walsh asks us to bring you in, that's what we'll do."

"I guess that's reasonable."

"Glad you think so," the man said blandly. "This here's your room." With that, the guide kicked open the door closest to him, turned his back on Clint, and walked away.

The room was comfortable, but not anything too special. It had all the basic amenities, including a bed, washbasin, dresser, and chair. There was a window, but the only things outside it were a plain stretch of brushy land and a barn. Just as Clint was about to look away, he spotted a familiar friend just outside that barn.

Nobody got in his way as he went outside to where

Eclipse was being led into the barn. "I'll take him from here," Clint said as he took the reins from the hand of a boy in his teens with a pockmarked face.

"Any stall in there you like," the kid said as he waved toward the barn. "Just don't move anyone else's horse."

That kid was a lot like the rest of the men. It wasn't so much that they were rude or angry with Clint in particular. It seemed more like they were just plain tired.

After getting Eclipse squared away, Clint slung his saddlebags over his shoulder and made his way back to his room. It was only late in the afternoon, but it felt closer to the end of a long evening. The air on Walsh's side of the fence just seemed a bit heavier. On the other hand, Livingston's side was charged with more nervous energy.

Clint rubbed his face with both hands and decided that he preferred to be somewhere far away from that fence if he had his choice. He wasn't too worried about being held prisoner or hunted down should he leave, but he didn't want to ride away just yet.

There was some unfinished business between these two brothers that Clint knew he could put to good use. At the most, he could end a feud that had torn a family apart and gotten some men killed in the process. At the least, he could offer his services and do whatever good he could manage.

For the moment, he had a roof over his head and what smelled like some good food on the way. And if he'd read these two brothers correctly, there was plenty more to be gained by someone who was smart enough to go after it.

Clint let out a breath and sat down upon his narrow bed. "All good things to those who wait."

SIXTEEN

Emmett Livingston strutted around his home like a king in his castle. He wore a newly made suit with a hat that was all the rage in Paris to act as his crown. The smirk on his lips was something new to a lot of the workers he passed. The friendly greeting from the Englishman was enough to make people think they were seeing a very talented imposter posing as the sour man who normally paid their wages.

"Hello there, young man," Livingston said to the next kid to cross his path.

Will stopped short and looked around to make sure he was the one Livingston had been talking to. Even when he saw there was nobody else in the man's line of sight, the kid still looked confused. "Umm . . . hello, Mr. Livingston."

"Fine day, isn't it?"

"Sure, I guess."

"I suppose my guest is finishing up his lunch?"

Will started to glance around as if he was now certain that he was in the wrong conversation.

Patting the kid on the shoulder, Livingston said, "Mr. Adams. You know him, right?"

"Oh, yeah!"

"Did he have his lunch?"

"I don't . . . think so."

Livingston was beginning to lose his patience, and caught himself before tightening his grip on the kid. "Is he in his room?"

"No."

"Fine." With that, Livingston pushed the kid aside and headed for the stairs. He took them two at a time and strode all the way down to where Clint had been staying. The door was ajar, so he pushed it open and stepped inside.

When he saw nothing but empty space, he stopped short.

"Excuse me, Mr. Livingston," Claudia said as she pushed past him and went into the room. She was straightening up the place without paying much mind to Livingston, himself.

"Where is he?" he asked.

"You mean Clint?"

"Yes. Where is he?"

Although the answer leapt into her mind, Claudia knew better than to just spit it out. In fact, anyone who could have seen the look in Livingston's eyes would know better than to say anything but what he wanted to hear unless they wanted to deal with the hell that was to follow.

"I'm not sure," was the answer she decided upon.

"You've been with him, haven't you?"

Hearing that caused Claudia's stomach to tighten. She wasn't sure what Livingston would say if he knew just how much she'd been with Clint. She guessed it wouldn't be good. "I . . . umm . . ."

"You've seen him up here. You've cleaned his room. I assume you've brought him water or the like," Livingston sputtered.

"Oh, yes. I've done all that."

"Didn't he ever talk to you?"

"Sure."

"Did he mention anything about leaving?"

Claudia took a moment to put on a confused expression, and started vaguely shaking her head. That was enough to push Livingston into a frenzy as he stormed out of the room and slammed the door behind him. In the space of a heartbeat, he shoved the door open again and glared angrily at Claudia.

"Find Adams," Livingston commanded. "Tell him I want to speak to him. And if you hear anyone else mention him, tell them to come to me."

"I will, sir."

"If anyone needs me, I'll be at one of the bunkhouses. Surely one of those men can remember something about his whereabouts."

Livingston stared so hard at her that it seemed he was trying to burn holes through the back of her head. "You sure you don't know where he went?" he asked. "I heard you came up here last night."

"That was just to fix his bed."

"If I find out you're lying—"

"Why would I lie about that?"

After a few moments, Livingston nodded. "All right, then. Just remember what I told you." With that, he stepped out of the room once more and stomped down the hall.

Only after she heard him go down the stairs did Claudia let out the breath she'd been holding. She then quickly finished what needed to be done and got the hell away from that room.

Livingston burned a trail through his home and then set his sights outside it. His first stop was the first bunkhouse, where he got plenty of peculiar glances from his men. Since it wasn't payday, and there were no shots flying through the air, they couldn't figure out what he was doing there.

After quickly asking a few of the men he did recognize,

Livingston hurried from the bunkhouse and made a quick tour of the area. A little while later, he was once again stomping into the large house at the middle of his property.

The only person to stand in his way was a tall woman with long, wavy brown hair. She had been a blonde a few years ago, but her hair had shifted to a darker color the more time she spent with Emmett Livingston. That wasn't exactly a bad thing, however. She was a definite beauty with a smile that didn't even falter when she fell under Livingston's angry gaze.

"What's the matter, darling?" she asked. "You look upset."

"Upset?" Livingston asked as he wheeled around to face her. Even though he might have felt like raising a hand to his wife throughout their marriage, he'd never actually followed through on it. "I am upset, Meredith. How bloody good of you to notice."

"What is it?"

As always, the woman's disposition had a calming effect upon her husband. Livingston couldn't exactly look at Meredith's rosy cheeks, pretty eyes, and easy smile while still holding onto whatever it was that made him upset. Looking at her ample figure and long legs, on the other hand, had a completely different effect upon him.

"It's Adams," he said. "I don't know where he is."

Meredith furrowed her brow and placed her hands upon her hips. "Adams? Is he one of the men you hired?"

"Yes. Quite a well-known one, actually."

"Oh, is he that gunfighter? The Blacksmith?"

"The Gunsmith, darling. Yes, that's him."

"I can help look for him if you like."

Livingston let out a long sigh before plastering on half a smile and saying, "Yes, darling. I would like that very much."

Up to a few minutes ago, Livingston had felt like the king in his castle. Not only had he had a plan for getting rid of his brother, but he'd even had the superior firepower to ensure his position. All he'd needed was a little more time to put everything in motion. Now, one of his most valuable pieces was no longer on the board.

Meredith, on the other hand, waved back at him as she went joyfully about her newly appointed task.

"Stupid cow," Livingston muttered.

SEVENTEEN

Clint spent a good amount of time taking a walk around Walsh's property. Although he wasn't under lock and key and didn't have anyone acting as a guard for him, he noticed there was always someone nearby to keep an eye on him. Since he didn't plan on going too far anyhow, Clint let himself be followed for as long as those men wanted to keep up with him.

The main thing Clint wanted to do was see what kind of operation Walsh was running. His first instincts had told him that Walsh was being fairly straightforward with him, and in the time that Clint took to check things out, he found nothing to dispute that.

The place was a functioning ranch with all the things that went along with it. There were plenty of places for things to be hidden, but Clint's gut told him that he probably wouldn't find much of anything if he looked. As he walked the grounds, he also thought about what Walsh had told him regarding his family history.

And the more he thought about all of that, the more everything seemed to fit together. Although it was an extreme circumstance, Walsh and Livingston did seem to fight like two brothers who'd been at each other's throats for years.

Shots had been fired and some blood had been spilt, but neither of them were taking the steps needed to truly bury the other. Unfortunately, the same couldn't be said for the men in the brothers' employ. Those men were getting hurt and a few had been killed. The fact that neither of the brothers seemed to give it that much thought told Clint a whole lot.

While he was thinking about those men on Walsh's payroll, Clint just happened to spot a few of them walking straight toward him. He spotted three at first, but two more soon fell into step with them. Clint hadn't seen exactly where they'd come from, so he assumed there were more nearby. All he needed to see was the intent look in those men's eyes to know they weren't about to welcome him to the ranch.

Clint kept walking casually from one building to another. Rather than take in the place as a whole, he was now looking for a specific spot where he didn't have to worry about getting ambushed from every side. Once he found a large set of stables with no doors or open windows on one side, Clint put his back to that wall and faced the group of men.

"Hello," Clint said amiably. "Nice day for a stroll."

All five men stopped within five or six paces of where Clint was standing. They fanned out so they were practically sealing Clint within a semicircle of holstered pistols.

That was never a good sign.

"What are you doing here?" the man at the middle of the group asked. He was a few inches shorter than Clint, with a thin goatee on his face. The top of his head was completely bald, which made it that much easier to spot the creases and scars that marred his scalp.

Shrugging, Clint replied, "Like I said. Just out for a walk."

One of the men next to the bald one leaned forward and sneered, "No. What are you doing *here*?"

Reaching out to hold the man next to him back, the bald one explained, "What my friend here wants to know is why you're at this ranch."

"I came to have a word with Mr. Walsh."

"You had your words. Why are you still here?"

"Fuck this," the second man grunted. Before he could say another word, he was silenced by a harsh glare from the bald man.

"Rick here's a little anxious," the bald man explained to Clint. "Actually, we all are."

"That's a shame," Clint said as he slowly shifted his eyes to stare down each man in turn. "Being overly anxious can get someone into a whole lot of trouble."

While four of the men either steeled themselves or eased back under Clint's gaze, the bald one wasn't as affected.

"You're right about that," the bald man said. "Maybe that's what got Davis into so much trouble."

"Which one of you is Davis?"

"Oh, none of us is Davis. He's dead."

Rick leaned forward again with a sneer on his lips and said, "You know that, you bastard, since you killed him."

All of the men stood by and watched Clint carefully. Their hands were moving toward their guns. They were all close enough to Clint for them to try to see, as the age-old saying had it, if they were good enough to hit the broad side of a barn.

Unfortunately, Clint just happened to be standing with his back to that broad side.

EIGHTEEN

"I've never met any of you men," Clint said evenly. "And I don't recall your friend Davis."

Grinning, the bald man said, "That's not much of a surprise. From what I hear, you're real good at shooting without giving a damn who's on the other end of it."

"Did you see me shoot your friend?"

"No. We heard you was bragging about it so much that it ain't no secret. Everyone knows The Gunsmith's working for that Englishman. Just like we already know you're claiming to be The Gunsmith."

If there was a big reason for Clint to have come all this way to stop someone from using his name, this was it. Actually, the main reason for him to come all this way was to keep things from getting this far. Now he was stuck in the very situation he'd been trying to avoid.

"Look," Clint said. "Men drop my name every day. I'm supposed to have been killed more times than I can count, but that doesn't mean that rumor is true."

"That won't be a rumor for long," the bald man said. "That's gonna be a cold, hard fact."

"First, why don't you ask yourself a question? Why don't you men ask yourselves why I would come here and

73

walk around alone like this if I'd killed a friend of your?
Doesn't that seem foolish?"

"I say we don't listen to a damn word he says, Pardee,"
Rick snarled. "I say we do what needs to be done without
any more talk."

Pardee didn't flinch. His eyes remained fixed on their
target and his expression seemed as etched deeply into him
as the scars that marked his bald head. "You telling me you
didn't work for the Englishman?"

Clint nodded.

"Then why did this man next to me escort you to Mr.
Walsh's place after you crossed the Englishman's fence?"
When he asked that question, Pardee nodded his bald head
toward the man on his other side.

Clint recognized that man as one of the riders who'd led
him through Walsh's property and right to his front door.

"I was at Livingston's place," Clint explained. "That
doesn't mean I was working for him. And it sure doesn't
mean I killed the man you say I did."

Pardee remained motionless. Around him, the men
shifted on their feet as their patience drained from them
like water from a cracked bucket.

"In the end, it don't much matter what you say," Pardee
explained. "You're one of Livingston's boys and that puts
you on the wrong side of this fight. Someone needs to pay
for what happened to Davis. Might as well be you."

As he said that, Pardee lunged forward. The rest of the
men with him were more than willing to follow suit.

Since it was too late to avoid the fight, Clint did the next
best thing and threw himself headfirst into it. Most of the
men seemed to be counting on backing him up against the
wall and didn't expect to see him charge straight down
their throats.

Rick had been itching for the fight the most, so he was
closest to Clint. Before he could draw his gun, he felt Clint

slam a quick fist into his gut as he darted past. The punch didn't do a lot of damage, but it caught Rick by surprise.

As soon as he was past Rick, Clint spun on the balls of his feet to face the first man who was quick enough to track his movements. That happened to be the man to Rick's right side. It was also the man that was now closest to where Clint was standing.

Clint heard the faint sound of iron brushing against steel. Under normal circumstances, he might not have picked up on that sound. Since that sound now meant a gun was being drawn, Clint didn't have any trouble distinguishing it from the rest.

Reaching out with a speed that put the others to shame, Clint snagged the gun from the closest man's holster and took it away from him. With a flick of his wrist, Clint tossed the gun away and shifted his attention to the next man.

Behind Clint, one of the others balled up a fist and slammed it into the small of Clint's back. A sharp, stabbing pain exploded in Clint's innards, forcing him to clench his teeth and spin around before that pain got any worse.

Clint found himself face-to-face with one of the men who'd escorted him onto Walsh's property. Before, the man had been cold and aloof. Now, he wanted Clint dead. That much was made perfectly clear just by looking into his eyes and reading the hatred there.

Before Clint could do anything about it, he felt another pain in his gut. This time, the man in front of him had snapped a punch into his stomach with his right hand. His left hand was in the process of lifting a pistol from its holster.

Rather than try to keep himself from being punched again, Clint concerned himself with the gun in the man's hand. He knew the others would have drawn their own weapons by now, which meant it was only a matter of time before the lead started to fly.

Clint's hand wrapped around the other man's wrist. He

pulled the man's gun arm up sharply and twisted just enough to get the finger on that trigger caught up inside the trigger guard. Sure enough, the other man let out a pained grunt as his finger was brought to the brink of snapping.

Instead of breaking the man's finger, Clint kept twisting his upper body while forcing the man off balance. That way, he brought himself around to look at what the others were doing while bringing the gunman along for the ride.

Clint had less than a second to look at his surroundings. In that time, he saw that Rick had replaced his gun with a knife and the others had circled around so each of them could get a clear shot at Clint. Pardee and one other had their guns raised and were about to start shooting.

Wrapping his arm even tighter around the gunman's captured limb, Clint stuck his own finger on the gun in the man's hand. There was another pained howl and a muted crunch as the man's arm was wrenched even further, but Clint ignored those things as he twisted the man's arm so he could take better aim.

It wasn't the most comfortable shot he'd ever taken, but Clint was close enough to his targets to pull that trigger with confidence. The gun barked three times in quick succession. The first shot gouged a bloody trench down the length of Pardee's arm. The second sent sparks flying from the blade of Rick's knife and the third hissed through the air in a spot that sent two others diving for cover.

One more painful twist allowed Clint to take the gun from its owner completely, and another flash of motion put his own modified Colt into his free hand. When he came to a stop, Clint was standing with his shoulders squared to the group of men and a gun in each hand.

"All right," Clint said. "Do you men still want to see this through, or would you rather take my word that I'm not the man you're after?"

Although there was still some fire in their eyes, the men looked over to Pardee before jumping into another fight.

Pardee had his gun drawn and was sighting on Clint, but he still didn't look too anxious to fire since he was staring down the barrel of one of the guns Clint held.

"Watch your step," was all Pardee said. After that, he holstered his gun and turned his back on Clint. When he walked away, the rest of the men grudgingly followed.

The man whose gun had been taken from him kept his eyes on Clint. When Clint tossed the borrowed gun back toward its owner, he had to fight from laughing when the man tried to catch it. The man's finger was either sprained or broken, because he nearly dropped his gun onto his own foot when he attempted to grab it.

After scooping up his pistol, the man holstered it and ran to catch up with the others like a dog with its tail between its legs.

NINETEEN

Life on either side of that barbed-wire fence was anything but quiet. Throughout the last several weeks, shootings, raids, and all sorts of trouble had become common practice. It was all to be expected with so many hired guns waiting around for something to shoot. More often than not, the men had taken to shooting at each other in senseless fights, or at whatever critters were stupid enough to wander so close to the bunkhouses.

When he heard the door slam behind him, Wade's first thought was that another scuffle among the men had led to gunplay. When he heard the footsteps inside his own room, he drew his gun and turned toward the door in a smooth, fluid motion.

"What's wrong with you?" Wade grunted to the person who'd stormed into his room. "You trying to get yourself shot?"

Although she was surprised to find herself at gunpoint upon entering the room, Meredith Livingston didn't seem to mind it too much. She held her hands out and glanced up from the barrel of Wade's gun to his cold eyes.

"My husband owns everything for miles in every direction," she said. "I don't need to be invited anywhere."

"That holds up so long as your husband is around," Wade said without holstering the gun. "You might want to think twice before thinking everything like that applies the same to wives."

As she slowly walked forward, the little smirk on Meredith's face grew. Her hands remained open, but she brought them together until she was able to gently close them around the barrel of Wade's gun. "My husband isn't here," she whispered. "And that's how I like it."

Wade looked down at the way she slowly moved her fingers up and down along the barrel of his gun. He kept his finger on the trigger, knowing the effect it would have upon her. Sure enough, she pulled in a quick, excited breath as he pointed the gun up as if to aim at the bottom of her chin.

"You're a peculiar woman, Mrs. Livingston."

She grinned and eased her hands along the gun until she could stroke Wade's wrist. "At least you see that I am a woman. That's a hell of a lot more than my husband can manage."

"With all this shooting that's been going on, I would have thought you'd be enjoying yourself."

"I like the excitement. The only problem is that when I get all worked up, I need something to do. Just knowing that you're right in the middle of everything when the shooting starts, it just gets my blood boiling."

Wade swung his feet down from where they'd been propped up on the sill of his window. As he stood up and turned to face Meredith, he kept his gun drawn and pointed at her. Even as he stepped in close to her, he pressed the gun's barrel gently against her stomach.

She closed her eyes and leaned her head back as if she was enjoying a hot bath. Her hands drifted away from Wade's wrists and down to his waist. Before much longer, she was slipping her hands between his legs so she could feel the erection that was growing there.

"Seems like you're enjoying this as much as I am," she purred.

Wade's eyes drifted along the side of Meredith's neck. Her skin was soft and smelled like rosewater. Her brown hair looked almost blond in the light that streamed in through the window. When she stroked his penis through his pants, she curled her full lips into a smile.

"I always enjoy your visits, Mrs. Livingston," he said, knowing how much she liked it when he called her by such a formal name. "But I told you it wouldn't be such a good idea for you to come by so often."

"Are you scolding me? You know how much I love that."

Easing the gun down, Wade slipped it back into its holster so he could put both hands on Meredith's waist. Her hips wriggled back and forth under her expensive dress as she moved close enough to brush against the front of his jeans.

"There's a lot of commotion around here," Wade forced himself to say. "I might need to go soon."

But Meredith was already unbuckling Wade's belt and slipping her hand into his pants. When she got her fingers around his cock, she smiled like a little girl who'd found there was one more cookie in the jar. "The commotion is from my husband. He's looking for you."

"Yeah? Maybe I should—"

Meredith placed her other hand flat upon his chest as if she was about to shove him down. Her first hand was stroking him up and down, working his rigid pole until it was as hard as she wanted. "He's looking, but I found you first," she whispered while lowering herself to her knees.

Wade knew better than to fight her. Once her mouth found the tip of his cock, the last thing he wanted to do was fight.

TWENTY

Meredith peeled off Wade's jeans without taking his cock from her mouth. She bobbed her head back and forth while stripping off his pants and pulling open his shirt. In a matter of seconds, she slid her hands up and down along his legs while sucking on him like a stick of candy.

Wade felt his legs going weak as she worked on him. Meredith was very talented with what she was doing, and knew how to send chills along a man's spine. Her lips wrapped tightly around him as her tongue slid along the bottom of his shaft. When he was just about to slide out of her mouth, he could feel her teeth brushing ever so slightly against him.

That bit of danger put a grin on his face that was similar to the one on hers when she'd been feeling his gun against her midsection. Now, her fingers stroked the inside of his legs as well as between them with the same loving attention she'd showed to that pistol.

She let him ease out of her mouth while looking up at him, and asked, "You still want to leave?"

Rather than say anything, Wade reached down with both hands to pull Meredith back onto her feet. She smiled and giggled under her breath as he swung her around and lowered her onto the floor next to the bed. By the time he started pulling off her dress, she wasn't giggling. Instead, she was breathing heavily and squirming to get out of her clothes.

Wade slid her dress down to expose her full, rounded breasts. He couldn't wait to get the dress off her completely before cupping her breasts in both hands. Her nipples were already hard, and only got harder as he rubbed them against his palms. Keeping one hand on her breast, he used his other to pull her dress down past her hips.

Meredith's curves meant he had to work a bit more to get the dress off her. Of course, they also meant that she was more than worth the effort. After a few more seconds, she stood before him wearing nothing but the jewels around her neck and the boots that laced all the way up to her knees.

"Goddamn," Wade said as he let his eyes wander up and down over her body. "Your husband would want me dead if he knew about this, but I don't even care."

Lowering herself onto the bed, she replied, "Don't worry about my husband. He's too concerned about his mines and land to think about anything else."

She scooted back until her shoulders bumped against the headboard. Propping herself up a bit, Meredith placed her heels on the edge of the mattress and slowly eased her legs apart. As she revealed the soft blond hair between her legs, she slipped her fingers along the sensitive nub of her clitoris.

As much as Wade liked to watch her, he couldn't keep away one moment longer. He knelt on the bed between her legs and reached down to place his hands once more upon her breasts.

"Come here," she whispered. "And bring that gun with you." This time, her hands were wrapped around the pistol between Wade's legs. Meredith guided him to the moist lips of her vagina and let out a trembling sigh as he slid inside.

Wade backed up just enough for him to stand at bedside and look down at her naked body. He took hold of Meredith's legs and roughly pulled her closer. She let out a little squeal as she was dragged so that her backside was on the edge of the mattress.

Keeping hold of her legs, Wade stepped forward and entered her once more. His hands were wrapped around Meredith's thighs, positioning her legs so both of them were against his chest and pointed straight up toward the ceiling.

Meredith smiled and arched her back, allowing Wade to move her wherever he wanted. Feeling him thrust in and out of her was more than enough to keep that smile on her face. In fact, she opened her legs a bit more and pumped her hips in time to his movements. That was more than enough to make her smile even wider.

Wade slid his hands up and down along the curves of Meredith's legs. The muscles in her thighs tightened every time he drove into her. They loosened a bit as he pulled out, but he could feel that she was anxious for the next thrust.

After a few minutes, Meredith squirmed away from him and rolled onto her knees. She was breathing heavily as she crawled on the bed and put her back to him. Tossing her hair over her shoulder, she looked back at Wade while lowering her front and arching her back.

"Come on, cowboy," she said in a breathy voice. "Take me for a ride."

Wade settled behind her and took her hips in both hands. "Yes, ma'am," he said as he slid his cock between her legs and plunged into her warm pussy.

She swallowed him up easily, enveloping every inch of him in a moist embrace. As he thrust his hips forward, Wade pulled hers back, allowing him to plunge into her deeper than he could from any other angle.

When Meredith let out her next breath, she couldn't help but let a moan out with it. Her hands clenched around the sheets and she lowered her head so her hair fell around her face like a curtain. Her entire body rocked back and forth as Wade pumped into her. The tighter she felt his hands clench her hips, the wetter her pussy became.

Shifting his hands to the small of her back, Wade kept pumping into her using his hips. With one hand, he traced a line along the slope of her spine. He used his other hand to rub the two little dimples just above the curve of her buttocks. Those dimples were Wade's favorite part of her body. Not only were they perfectly spaced in a section of silky smooth skin, but seeing them meant he was doing exactly what he was doing now.

He kept his hand on those dimples and reached out with his other to take a fistful of Meredith's hair. He pulled her head back as he buried his cock inside her, which filled the room with her excited moans. Soon, his voice mingled with hers as the bed took its last few knocks against the wall.

TWENTY-ONE

"Where do you think you're going?" Walsh shouted as he stomped out of the front door of his house.

Clint had Eclipse saddled and loaded up with everything he'd brought over the fence. "I'm leaving this property," he replied. "And if you try to tell me you don't know why, I won't believe a word of it."

"Look, I know my men acted out of turn. That doesn't mean we can't help each other."

"This is becoming more trouble than it's worth."

"If you truly believed that, you never would have bothered in the first place." When he saw Clint pause rather than snap his reins and ride away, Walsh pounced on the moment. "At the very least, hear me out. We don't have to talk here if you don't want to."

"All right," Clint said. "How fast can you get a horse?"

"A few minutes."

"As soon as you get one, start riding east."

"For how long?"

"Until I find you. And don't bring anyone with you. I'll know if you do." With that, Clint pointed Eclipse toward the north and snapped the reins. The Darley Arabian took off fast enough to breeze past anyone who got in his way.

By the time the few others out there tried to take a second look at the racing stallion, Eclipse was gone.

There wasn't much in the northern section of Walsh's land. With a hearty portion of his herd on one drive or another, the grazing land was sparsely populated by a few head of cattle and plenty of jackrabbits. Walsh rode east at a steady pace while keeping his eye on the horizon.

It had taken some convincing, but he was alone. That is, unless the gun at his hip and on his saddle weren't counted as escorts. Walsh wouldn't have been stupid enough to leave his house without those companions.

Soon, he heard what sounded like a bit of thunder in the distance. When he turned to get a look in that direction, he saw the black Darley Arabian charging toward him at full steam. The horse slowed quickly and came to a stop next to Walsh's gelding.

Eclipse was breathing heavily enough for steam to come from his nostrils, but it was the gelding who appeared to be more shaken by the entrance.

"I was told about what happened," Walsh said. "I didn't order it."

Clint nodded. "I figured as much. Still, I thought it would be a good idea to continue our business without ruffling any more feathers. It was my mistake to stay there since your men thought I shot their friend."

"Testing the waters didn't hurt, though."

Studying Walsh for a few seconds was enough for Clint to see the intelligent spark in the man's eyes. He'd hit that nail on the head with almost as much ease as he'd figured Clint was the genuine Gunsmith and not some loudmouth from a saloon.

"Those men have plenty of fire in their bellies," Clint said. "If they're still this ready for a fight, they'll find a way to get one sooner rather than later."

"It's going to be sooner. I can tell you that much for certain."

"That is, unless this is ended before they get a chance."

"And how would you propose on doing that? My brother isn't exactly ready to listen to reason."

"Sometimes, one thing can change the tide of a war," Clint explained. "One thing may change a man's life. It may also change two men's lives, despite how stubborn they both are."

"And you've got something in mind?"

"Yeah. I do."

Walsh shook his head slowly and said, "Pardon my manners, but I have a hard time believing that one thing could turn this around."

"Maybe not all the way, but it could be enough to turn things in the right direction."

"And why would you put so much effort into this? I know I asked you something like that before, but since then you've been attacked by my men and been shown that this is undoubtedly a bigger mess than you could have guessed."

"This has been a mess," Clint replied. "And a dangerous one. But it's the dangerous jobs that usually pay the best."

Walsh nodded and smiled a bit. "Ah, you want money. I should have guessed."

"I'm not out to cheat anyone, and I'm certainly not about to put a dent in your inheritance. But seeing all the men you've been paying to stand around and look tough, I think it's fair to be paid for the service I'm offering."

After a few seconds, Walsh grinned. "A man's got to eat."

"That's right."

Keeping his grin intact, Walsh added, "I've heard plenty of things about you as well, Adams. One of them is that you've helped a lot of people, done a lot of good, without asking for a dime in return."

"You heard that right. Folks who are forced into a hard

place and can't find a way out deserve all the help a man can give. But I've done plenty of looking into this situation, Mr. Walsh. It's a rough spot, but it's not exactly some terrible situation that was dropped on you or your brother's head. You dug yourselves into this hole after years of being assholes. I figure you're rich enough to pay to get yourself out."

"I have paid," Walsh said grimly. "And not with just those gun-toting cowboys you met. You're absolutely right, Adams. I've paid plenty. There's no reason not to pay a little more. But," he added, "only if there's results."

"I wouldn't accept a dime otherwise."

"Sounds fair. Now let's hear this plan of yours."

TWENTY-TWO

Livingston was beside himself. He sat in his saddle like he was riding a polo pony, but the scowl on his face looked more like he was in the middle of a war. A few beads of sweat trickled down his brow after a day filled with a whole lot of riding and plenty of yelling at his own men. When he saw one of those men riding toward him, he waited for him to get close enough to hear the sound of his raised voice.

But the rider was first to start yelling. Without pulling back on the reins, he shouted, "I found him! I found him!"

"Who did you find?" Livingston asked once the rider had finally drawn up close and slowed his horse down.

"That Gunsmith fella. I found him."

"Where was he?"

"A few acres out. Not far from here."

"And why didn't anyone find him until now?"

Knowing there was no way for him to answer that question without getting Livingston riled up, the rider simply shrugged and shook his head.

"Well, bring him to my study," Livingston ordered.

"Yes, sir!" The rider was more than happy to turn back around and head out the way he'd come. He was gone amid

a flurry of hooves, leaving Livingston to sulk all the way
back to his house.

When he got back, Livingston threw open the front door
and stalked all the way through the mansion and into the
study. He headed straight for a brandy snifter and poured
himself a healthy dose of liquor. When he turned and
tipped back the glass, he spotted his wife reclining in one
of the many overstuffed chairs.

"How long have you been there?" Livingston asked.
"And why are you smiling like the cat that swallowed the
mouse?"

"I'm just enjoying the day. Is there a law against that?"

"No. And thank you for helping me in the one thing I
asked you to do, by the way."

She shrugged and shifted in her seat. One hand was
wrapped around a crystal wine glass and the other played
with a few strands of her hair. "Oh, I found your precious
gunfighter," she said.

"You did? How long ago was this?"

"An hour. Maybe two."

"Wonderful," Livingston grunted with a scowl. "And I
suppose you just let him ride off afterward?"

"I told him you wanted to speak to him, but assumed he
was free to go where he pleased. I wasn't instructed to tie
him up and drag him here. You have plenty of gunmen to
do that sort of thing for you."

"Yes," Livingston said as he watched his wife carefully.
"But I figured you wouldn't mind doing that task yourself."

Her only response to that was a little shrug as she took
another sip of wine.

"One of my men has done what I asked," Livingston continued. "So if you don't mind, take your drink elsewhere."

"Why are you always so mean to me?"

"Stop your pouting. You live like the Queen herself.
Now take your royal self somewhere else, if you please."

She stood up and put an undeniably sexy pout on her

face. Approaching her husband slowly, she didn't stop until she was literally nose to nose with him. Reaching down with one hand, she massaged him between his legs until she felt an erection start to grow there.

"I'll leave you in peace," she whispered. "But only after a kiss."

"Honestly, Meredith."

Her hand continued to rub him. Once she felt him become harder, she rubbed him even more vigorously until she could hear his breath speeding up. "I could take care of you here," she offered. "Just like you like it. Doesn't that always help you relax? I'd say you need it."

Livingston closed his eyes for a second and let out a slow breath. Reluctantly, he took hold of her wrist and moved her hand from between his legs. "Later, perhaps." He kissed her on the lips and then kissed her again. Although the second one was somewhat more passionate, neither kiss put a flush in Meredith's cheeks.

"They'll be here any minute," he said as he all but pushed her away. "Wait for me in our bedroom and we can finish this business then."

"Fine, but I can't promise that I won't finish it on my own." With that, she turned and strutted from the study.

Livingston watched his wife leave, thinking back to the days when their marriage had been fresh and exciting. He could still taste her on his lips, but even that didn't make him as happy as it once did. In fact, these days, it was quite the opposite.

TWENTY-THREE

Once more, Clint was brought across a large stretch of private land by an armed escort. Unlike the last few times, he didn't pay much attention to the guns around him or the men carrying them. Those hired guns were just a part of the scenery as far as he was concerned. Where the two brothers were concerned, that was one of the biggest problems.

Livingston was waiting for Clint in his study. Rather than expend any effort in checking the lay of the land or the spread itself, Clint rode right up to the house and walked straight to where its owner was waiting.

"I've been wondering where you went," Livingston said. "When I saw your room was empty, I feared the worst."

"I went across the fence to pay Walsh a visit."

Livingston's face dropped and his hand started to inch toward the gun at his side. "Why would you do that?"

"If I'm to help you out of this mess, I thought I should get to know who I'm up against. The men you hired may be able to fire a shot or two, but they're not much for thinking things through."

"I don't pay them for that," Livingston said as if he was reading it from a script. "Perhaps that's a problem."

92

"I spoke to Mr. Walsh."

"And you managed to get out of there alive? I'm surprised."

"I did catch a little hell, but things could have been worse."

This time, Livingston smiled. "He's an unreasonable, selfish idiot."

Clint had to fight back the urge to bring up family similarities, but somehow managed to bite his tongue. "I got a good look at his operation. He's got plenty of men, but they're unorganized, rowdy, and have itchy trigger fingers."

"I've figured out some of that for myself."

"But you obviously haven't figured out how all of those things can play to our advantage."

"Expert tactics, eh?" Livingston said as he perched upon the edge of his seat. "Keep talking."

"I'm set to lay it all out for you," Clint replied. "I'm also prepared to carry out the roughest portions of the plan myself. That's the only way to be certain things get done right. Considering how long you've been struggling with this problem, I figured you'd want it wrapped up nice and neat."

Nodding quickly, Livingston said, "Most definitely."

"After seeing both sides of the fence for myself, it's obvious that you're the one with the most resources and the most legitimate claim to winning this dispute."

"That's so refreshing to hear from a third party. Especially since you very well have chosen whichever best suits your needs."

Clint shrugged. "Picking the winning side of a fight suits anyone's needs."

"But you could have chosen to steer clear of this fight altogether," Livingston pointed out.

"A man like me doesn't succeed by passing up opportunities like this. You're a businessman, so you know just as well as I do that we take full advantage of whatever comes our way. This is the best type of venture, Mr. Livingston. It's one where both you and I can come out ahead."

"And I assume you won't be doing this out of the kindness of your heart?"

Clint smiled. "I may be offering my services to the best side, but I'm still putting my neck on the line. The men you've hired haven't gotten the job done. All you need is someone who truly knows what they're doing, has a plan, and has the talent to see it through. You and Mr. Walsh may be butting heads until the end of days, but wars of attrition are long and messy. You don't have to look too far back into this country's own history to see that much."

"Indeed," Livingston said with a wince.

"What I'm offering is a quick end to this war. That way, the killings will stop, everyone can get on with their lives, and the world can keep on spinning. How's that sound?"

"Fine, but you still haven't named your fee."

"Two thousand should cover it. Considering all that you're paying to keep those hired guns fed and housed, that shouldn't be too bad. Besides, winning your war with Walsh should allow you to cover that much in no time at all."

Livingston nodded slowly while rubbing his chin. "As you said. Winners all around."

"So, you accept my offer?"

After a bit of contemplation, Livingston stood and stuck out his hand. "I do accept it, sir."

Before he shook the Englishman's hand, Clint added, "And I'm sure you would agree to paying half now with the other half to be delivered upon completion of the job?"

"I suppose we must trust each other somewhat for this to work."

"That would help."

Grudgingly, Livingston offered his hand a second time. "I can see the money gets into your hands now."

"Excellent," Clint said as he shook Livingston's hand.

The Englishman's grip was loose and clammy, which really wasn't much of a surprise.

After the deal was sealed, Livingston walked around his desk and pulled a section of rug up from the floor. Although Clint couldn't see exactly what the Englishman was doing, he could hear the sound of a metal dial being turned, followed by the groan of an iron door being opened.

When Livingston stood up again, he had one hand full of a neat stack of money. "You can count it if you like."

Clint took the money and flipped through it. "That won't be necessary," he said, even though he'd counted it with that single pass of his thumb over the bills.

"Good. Then I'd like to hear this plan of yours."

TWENTY-FOUR

The first part of Clint's plan for Livingston was to pick a spot to meet up with Walsh. Since Walsh wasn't an idiot, it would have to be a spot that would entice him to show, even though he would be suspicious. The idea was to bargain for a trade between something that Walsh wanted for something that Livingston wanted. From there, as Clint had explained it, both men would be able to lower their guard and start acting as business partners.

It was Livingston who first jumped on the chance to point out what a great time that would be to ambush Walsh. Clint shrugged and agreed to let the Englishman finish things however he'd wanted. The fact that Livingston was running down the path Clint had steered him toward was an unforeseen bonus.

One day was all it took for Livingston to pick his spot, send his message across the fence, and get his reply. Since Clint knew Walsh would be waiting for that message to arrive, it wasn't too much of a surprise that things were moving so smoothly. What did surprise him was how willing Livingston was to deal rather than ride out with every one of his gunmen.

When Clint and one other gunman were the only ones to

accompany Livingston out into his property, it seemed that the Englishman might be willing to see reason after all.

The three men rode across the southwestern expanse of Livingston's property. It was a particularly rough stretch of land with more rock than dirt under the horses' hooves. Every step the horses took rattled each rider down to the marrow in his bones. Just enough dust was kicked up by the horses to fill the air with a gritty silt.

Rather than try to be heard over the noise of the horses, Livingston pointed to a rocky hill less than half a mile in the distance. As they drew closer to that hill, Clint could see the large square opening in the side of it. Thick timbers framed the opening and two iron rails leading into the rock glinted in the sun.

Once the horses all came to a stop, the silt kicked up by their hooves swirled through the air to surround them in a gray cloud. Despite the fact that he owned that land, Livingston was the least accustomed to it. The Englishman pulled a handkerchief from his pocket and used it to cover his face until the dust settled.

"Is this the place?" Clint asked.

Livingston nodded.

The other man with them stood up in his stirrups and looked around. "I don't see anyone else."

"That—that's because we're early," Livingston coughed. "I've dealt with that bastard Walsh long enough to know better than trust he'll work strictly aboveboard."

Chuckling as he dug the spyglass from his saddlebag, Clint said, "You'd breathe in less dust if you weren't so long-winded."

The gunman started to laugh at that, but quickly stopped when he saw the embarrassed look on his boss's face.

"You're right, of course, Mr. Adams," Livingston said. "Old habits do tend to die hard."

Clint surveyed the horizon with his spyglass, concentrating in the direction of Walsh's property. "Nobody's

coming from his side of the fence just yet, but it is early."
Shifting in his saddle, Clint picked out a group of four riders coming from the south. "Hold on, now. I see someone."

"Are they headed this way?" the gunman asked.

Before Clint could respond, Livingston spit into his
handkerchief and dabbed at the corner of his mouth. "I told
you Walsh would try to send someone here before us. They
probably want to set up an ambush."

"We don't know that," Clint said. "But they are headed
this way."

"Damned Irishman," Livingston said. "He's been sending men to look for this mine for years. Now that he knows
where it is, he'll probably want to kill us and grab whatever
he can."

"Let's see who it is before we jump to conclusions,"
Clint said with confidence. "For all we know, it might be
one of your own—"

Before Clint could even finish that sentence, a shot was
fired from one of the approaching riders. The bullet was a
long way from hitting any of the three men outside the
mine entrance, but it came close enough to let them know
the intentions of the one who'd fired it.

"There's more of them coming," the gunman said.
"They're closing in from all sides!"

More shots ripped through the air, drawing closer with
every second. Although Clint couldn't see any more than
the first group of men that had been spotted, he could tell
that plenty more were on the way. "This wasn't supposed
to happen," Clint muttered.

"Yer damn right," the gunman replied. "Goddamn
Irishman!"

Clint didn't like the look of this one bit. Something had
gone seriously wrong somewhere along the line. What
bothered him even more was that he didn't know why. Before he could figure any of that out, however, he decided to
try and keep himself from getting shot.

TWENTY-FIVE

All three men had gotten off their horses and moved closer to the mine entrance. Although there might have been men coming over the hill, there wasn't any way for them to shoot through a rock wall and into the mine. For the moment, at least, the dark, musty shadows of the mine were their safest bet.

Clint took quick aim and fired a shot with his rifle. He knew he had enough range to hit the oncoming riders, but didn't want to draw any blood until he knew why all this was happening in the first place. "Get behind me!" he shouted.

Although Livingston was more than happy to oblige, the other gunman wasn't so willing. He'd drawn the rifle from his own saddle harness and was firing as quickly as he could pull the trigger.

"They split up, all right," the gunman said as he levered in a fresh round. "Two of 'em are coming from the other side!"

Clint squinted through the musty columns of light that had formed as beams from the sun passed through the thick curtains of dust. Sure enough, he could see two coming from one side of the mine along with another two coming from where he'd spotted the original group.

"Looks like that first group's just split up," Clint said. "There's probably not as many of them as we think."

"I don't much care how many there are," Livingston sputtered. "I'm more concerned that they're shooting at us!"

One bullet tore a piece from the wooden frame of the entrance and then sparked along the rock wall behind Clint. The whining echo filled the narrow entrance before fading into the depths of the shaft behind him. "This could still be a misunderstanding!" Clint said.

The gunman turned a set of disbelieving eyes toward Clint. "And what the hell makes you think that?"

There wasn't a way for Clint to answer that without tipping his hand, so he merely shook his head and fired another shot from his rifle.

"Whoever they are or whatever they think, they're getting closer," Livingston pointed out.

"And I doubt they'll be much for talking," said the gunman.

Clint squinted through the dust until he could make out the faces of the two riders coming straight toward the mine. When he got a clear look at one of their faces, he could hardly believe it. "That's not one of Walsh's men," he said.

"What?" Livingston said. "I'll just have to see about that!" Before anyone could do anything to stop him, the Englishman stormed away from the mine and headed straight into the line of fire.

Clint reached out to grab hold of Livingston's arm. "Where the hell do you think you're going?"

Even though Clint was able to snag a part of Livingston's sleeve, he wasn't able to keep the Englishman from leaving the entrance to the mine. That wasn't so much due to the other man's speed or agility as it was due to the way the gunman stepped in between them and aimed at Clint.

Pointing his gun straight at Clint's face, the gunman

shook his head slowly. Clint got the point, stepped back, and allowed Livingston to go wherever he meant to go.

"Hold your fire!" Livingston shouted as he ran away from the mine with his hands flailing over his head. "I said hold your fire!"

A few more shots cracked through the air around him, but those quickly tapered off and came to a stop. By the time Livingston had taken a few more steps, all four of the other riders had come forward.

Three of the men had hired on with Livingston less than a week ago. The fourth had been with him for a considerably longer stretch of time. It was that fourth one who came forward and stared at Livingston over the smoking barrels of his guns.

"Is that you, Mr. Livingston?" Wade asked. He had a pistol in each hand, and still looked as if he was going to fire them even as he approached his employer.

Livingston didn't have to dig too deeply to act frightened as he stumbled away from the mine. "It's me! It's me! Don't shoot!"

"How'd you get away?"

"I don't know, but I slipped off in the confusion. Good job with all of that."

The other three men nodded at Livingston's story, but Wade didn't seem as convinced. In fact, after a few quick glances, he didn't even seem to care the other three were even there.

"I was told you were being kidnapped," Wade said.

"So I was," Livingston replied. "Thanks to you, I managed to escape."

"Where are the ones who took you?"

"In there!" Livingston said while pointing with both hands toward the mine's entrance. "You'd better get after them before they get away."

Wade slowly climbed down from his saddle. He'd holstered one pistol to free up that hand, but kept his other pistol aimed at the mine. His eyes kept glancing back and forth between Livingston and that mine. "How many of them were there?"

"Three, I think."

"You think?"

"I didn't have time to count!" the Englishman said as the anger welled up in his voice. "I'm lucky to even be alive! Now are you going to keep questioning me, or are you going to do your job?"

"I'm here doing my job, Mr. Livingston," Wade said warily.

"Then do what I say and get after those bloody kidnappers!"

Letting out a measured breath, Wade walked toward the mine entrance. He stopped before crossing into the shadows and began to turn back around. Suddenly, he heard a voice explode from the mine, which got his heart slamming inside his chest once more.

With that voice still ringing in his ears, he heard more shots blast toward him. The first one came from within the mine, but the next barrage came from outside it. In fact, most of those shots were fired by the very same men who'd dragged him all the way out to that mine in the first place.

Wade turned on his heels and shouted to the men now gathered around Livingston. They were still firing wildly and wouldn't listen to a word Wade said. As the shots coming from inside the mine drew closer, Wade turned and fired in that direction.

Hunkering down low, Wade jumped to one side until his right shoulder bumped against the rock wall. He pulled his trigger several times in quick succession, illuminating the inside of the mine with a series of flickering sparks.

"Hold it!" shouted one of the men inside the mine.

Another voice echoed from within the darkness. This one said, "Shoot him!"

Wade kept from pulling the trigger just long enough to get a look at who was running out of the mine. He recognized the gunman as one of the new ones hired by Livingston. "What the hell's going on in there?"

The gunman pointed wildly over his shoulder. "There's a bunch of Walsh's boys in there and they aim to kill us!"

After the gunman had gone past him, Wade stared into the shadows. The next thing he felt was a shove against his back, which sent him sprawling into the mine. When he wheeled around to see who'd pushed him, he found himself staring down the barrels of over half-a-dozen drawn pistols outside the mine's entrance.

When he looked into the darkness once more, he saw Clint staggering toward him while rubbing the back of his head.

"I told you to shoot him," Clint groaned.

TWENTY-SIX

Wade couldn't decide which sight confused him more: Clint staggering toward him like he was a few sheets to the wind, or Livingston standing outside in the middle of a bunch of other men who'd ridden at his side for less than a week.

"What're you doing here, Adams?" Wade asked.

Clint took his hand from the back of his head and looked at it. His fingers and palm were slick with blood. The holster at his hip was empty. "Why don't you ask *them*?" Clint asked while nodding toward the men outside the mine.

The moment Wade made a move toward those other men, he was stopped by the sounds of every single pistol's hammer being snapped into firing position. Slamming his fist against the frame of the entrance out of sheer frustration, Wade snarled, "Someone tell me what the hell this is about or I'll shoot every last one of you!"

"Surely," Livingston said in a smug voice. "This is about men like yourselves who decide to take advantage of men like me in our weakest moment."

"Perhaps you should be a little clearer," Clint said.

"Ah, yes. For those of you in the dark."

Although a few of the men next to Livingston forced themselves to laugh, none of them could dredge up as much enthusiasm as the Englishman himself.

"Pardon my stinging sense of humor," Livingston said, "but I do find this to be a particularly satisfying moment."

Wade shook his head and looked at Clint. "What're you doing here, Adams? Or are you gonna talk circles around me as well?"

"I was hired on to help stop these assholes from shooting at each other and was brought here. We saw you and your friends coming. The next thing I knew, I had a gun in my face and was forced in here and knocked on the back of the head. That idiot out there couldn't even knock me out properly."

Wade laughed under his breath and turned to the rest of the men. "His story sounds about right. What about yours, Englishman?"

"I do admit to a bit of deception," Livingston replied. "Unfortunately, since I can't trust either of you at the moment, it was a necessary evil. Then again, if you'd like to know why you're both in there, perhaps you could ask my wife."

Clint wiped the blood off his hands using the edge of his shirt. The moment he touched the aching part of his head, however, he was smeared with blood once more. There was a dull pain in his skull, but he wasn't dizzy. At least there was some bit of good news.

"All right," Clint said after a few moments had passed. "I'll bite. What's your wife got to do with any of this?"

Livingston took a step forward. He was no longer smiling. "My wife is a beautiful woman. During all the years I've known Meredith, it's plain to see that I'm not the only one to appreciate her beauty. Unfortunately, some men are more civil when it comes to admiring her than others and that's led to plenty of misunderstandings.

"My wife is also not a lady in the traditional sense of

the word. I came to this uncomfortable realization when I saw the way she encouraged the looks she got from men." Livingston had come to a stop a few paces short of the mine's entrance. The men behind him had fanned out a bit so they could still keep Clint and Wade in their sights.

"Within the last few days," Livingston continued, "I've noticed something peculiar about Meredith." His voice had a definite edge to it and his eyes had narrowed down to angry slits. "She looked different. Rather like a little girl who'd managed to slip something past her father. She walked differently. It wasn't until we were alone in my den that I picked up on the one thing that made all the difference."

Taking a few more steps, Livingston clenched his fists and lowered his voice to a hiss. His eyes darted back and forth between Clint and Wade. He didn't even seem to take notice of the gun still in Wade's hand. "When we were alone that last time, I noticed she smelled differently. She'd been with a man. I could tell that much just by being close to her. I could smell it on her like she was just another dirty whore in a saloon."

"Sorry to hear that," Clint said. "What's this got to do with us?"

"I asked her what happened and she didn't even have the courtesy to deny what she'd done," Livingston explained. "She even told me who she'd taken into her bed. She held her head high and revealed she'd given herself to The Gunsmith, himself."

Clint shook his head, wincing at the pain that caused. "I was at Walsh's place."

"You should know better than to even think it was me," Wade said to Livingston. "If you know she was cheating on you, why would you even believe a damn word that came out of her mouth?"

"When I had this discussion with her, it was under . . . shall we say . . . extreme circumstances. By the time I was finished with her, she wasn't in the proper frame of mind to lie. Those were her last words, after all."

"What?" Clint snapped. "Did you hurt your own wife?"

"Only for a little bit. She's dead now, as well she should be. I won't lose a wink of sleep over the matter seeing as how she spread her legs for the likes of a known killer."

"This is crazy," Clint said as he started walking toward the entrance. "Your wife's probably just craving attention since you spend all your nights worrying about this stupid war with your brother."

"I told you, Mr. Adams," Livingston said as he snapped his fingers. "My wife is dead."

Hearing that snap, one of the men from behind Livingston tossed a large bundle into the mine. Clint could make out that the bundle was actually a load of dynamite connected to a set of wires leading behind Livingston.

When the Englishman stepped aside to reveal the plunger at the end of those wires, he added, "And soon, the both of you will be dead as well." After giving a quick, curt wave, Livingston stepped over to the detonator and pushed down on the plunger.

TWENTY-SEVEN

A lot of things raced through Clint's mind in the space of one second.

He thought back to whether or not he'd even met Meredith Livingston.

He wondered if the woman was truly dead.

He wondered if Livingston truly had the guts to toss a load of dynamite toward two men and set it off.

Fortunately, Clint's instincts didn't wonder about any such things. They were too busy getting his legs moving so he could dive for cover at the back of the tunnel. If the explosion never came, there would be time enough to feel foolish later.

But the explosion came.

In fact, it rocked the tunnel under Clint's feet, blinded him with a flash of light, and deafened him with a blast that sounded as if the world itself had cracked open underneath the weight of a giant hammer.

Clint bolted into the tunnel with his hands held out in front of him as his only guides. It seemed as if he was running for hours on end as the rumble of the explosion kept battering against his eardrums. At times, he didn't know whether he was still running or if he was falling. In the middle of that much chaos, nothing was certain.

The pain he'd felt from the blow to his head spread out to encompass his entire body as rocks dropped onto his head, back, and shoulders. Uneven ground caused him to twist his ankles and strain his knees so many times that his legs went numb. The dirt and dust were so thick in the air that every one of his breaths burned the back of his throat.

After what seemed like an eternity, Clint slowed down. It wasn't so much a conscious decision as it was a simple matter of running out of steam. He couldn't see his hand in front of his face, but he could feel the sweat and tears running down his cheeks. When he tried to wipe away the grit from his eyes, the burning only got worse.

There was still a rumbling going through the air, but the sound bounced off so many cramped tunnels that Clint swore he'd been buried alive. Unfortunately, as he thought back to what had just happened, that possibility didn't seem so farfetched.

Taking the bandanna from around his neck, Clint started wiping off his face and eyes. He ignored the burning and finally cleared away enough of the grit to confirm that he wasn't blind. Even so, there wasn't much to see apart from a few dark shapes against an even darker background.

"J-Jesus Christ."

Since he knew *he* didn't say that, Clint realized that he hadn't been alone in his race down the mine shaft. With every thump of his heart, more memories rushed back into his mind. Before too long, he felt like most everything in his skull was in its proper place after being rattled by that blast.

"That you, Wade?"

"I'm pretty sure it is. At least, what's left of me. How you doing, Adams?"

"Near as I can tell . . . not bad."

"I can't see," Wade grunted. "I think I got an eyeful of cinders and dust, though."

"Me, too. Hold on a second," Clint said as he dug around in his pockets. When he found what he'd been looking for, he waited and pulled in a few deep breaths through his nose. All he could smell was dirt and wet stone, so he struck one of the matches he'd found in his pocket against the nearest wall.

When the little spark blazed to life, it seemed like someone had just let the sun into the room through an open door. After a few seconds, Clint's eyes adjusted and the blazing light died down to the sputtering match that it was.

Wade was squinting hard enough to make it plain that his eyes were adjusting as well. A couple seconds after Clint's vision had settled down, Wade was able to open his eyes all the way as well.

They were in a roughly cut tunnel that was about an inch lower than the two men hunched down in it. The walls were supported here and there by wooden beams and a few of those beams even stretched across the ceiling. However, for every whole beam there was, there were two other beams that were cracked in at least two different places.

Clint swung his arm slowly in a circle so he could get a look at the tunnel without putting out the flame. There were tracks under their feet, which stuck up every couple of yards from beneath layers of dust, gravel, and cobwebs. Those tracks stretched ahead into a tunnel that appeared to branch off a little ways up.

Behind them, the tracks were buried in a pile of blackened rocks that were still shifting and settling in upon themselves. The smell of burnt dynamite hung in the air like a thick, suffocating cloud. Clint lifted the match to the ceiling, which showed him there was less than half an inch of space between the top of the rock pile and the top of the tunnel.

Wade stepped up and reached out to the top of the pile.

He placed one foot upon the pile for leverage, but quickly slipped as the rocks came loose underneath his boot. When he started to fall, Wade caught himself with a quickly outstretched arm and got another section of the rocks to tumble and shift noisily.

"Get away from there," Clint hissed as he took hold of Wade's collar and pulled him back.

"But it feels like these rocks are loose."

"Yeah, they're loose. They also might be the only thing holding the rest of this tunnel up."

"It might be worth the risk if that's the only way out of here," Wade said.

"I don't think it is. Look." As he said that, Clint held the match once again at the top of the pile. The flame sputtered, but remained lit as it worked its way right down to Clint's fingers. Shaking it out, Clint said, "There's no air coming through there. That either means the tunnel's completely blocked a few feet ahead or that it's sealed off altogether."

In the darkness, Wade let out a sigh.

TWENTY-EIGHT

"So," Wade grunted as he shuffled along the tunnel with the back of his head bumping against solid rock, "this is what the road to hell is like."

Clint was a few steps ahead of him, stretching out his arm a few feet over the floor. "Not quite. My guess is it's a lot hotter than this."

"Well, this sure must be close."

"For a man who wants to have folks think he's a famous gunfighter, you sure do whine a lot."

"And for a man who *is* a famous gunfighter, you sure did a piss-poor job of keeping yourself out of harm's way."

Clint was close to tossing down the match and taking a swing at Wade. The fact that there were only a few matches left from the ones he'd grabbed at Walsh's place was the only thing that kept him from doing just that. With that in mind, Clint hunkered down and looked even harder for something he could fashion into a torch.

"You sure this is the right way?" Wade asked. "It feels like these walls are getting closer in around us."

Shaking his head, Clint replied, "You're the one that's been working for Livingston longer, so you tell me. Haven't you gotten a look at this place before now?"

"Hell, no, I haven't. That Englishman holds onto his money tighter than he does that wife of his. All me or any of the other boys working for him have seen is what we can see from horseback."

Clint took another few steps and smiled as a cool rush of air washed over his face. It wasn't fresh air by any means, but there was enough of it to tell him that an open area was real close. Sure enough, a few more steps brought him into a cave the size of a small room.

"Ah," Wade breathed. "This is more like it."

The room was roughly square shaped and had tool marks on most every part of the walls. The edges were cluttered with trash and bits of junk that had obviously been cast aside by miners.

"Take a look around for a lantern," Clint said as he picked up a piece of lumber from a pile.

"Anything that could burn would be nice. My eyes feel like they're about to bleed after all that damn squinting."

"I'm one step ahead of you." With that, Clint touched the match to the end of the lumber he'd found. There wasn't much flame left in that match, but the lumber was dry enough to catch fire fairly easily. Although there was barely enough light to see by, Clint put his boot against a burlap sack and tore off a strip of it with his free hand. When he wrapped the burlap around the end of the lumber, it seemed as it he'd extinguished the flame. Before long, however, the burlap began to crackle and then a flame roared to life.

Wade's eyes widened at the sight of the burning torch. In a matter of seconds, he'd picked up a long hunk of lumber for himself and tore off another strip of burlap. Touching the lumber to Clint's torch was more than enough to set it ablaze and bathe the cave in a warm, shaky light.

"All right," Wade said triumphantly. "Now we're in business." He nodded as he took in the rest of the cave. A few of the larger piles caught his interest, so he went over there to sift through them. "Looks like some equipment in here," he reported. "We might be able to dig ourselves out after all."

When he glanced back at Clint, Wade didn't see the enthusiasm he'd expected. "What's wrong with you?"

Clint had lowered himself onto the floor so he could stretch his legs and straighten his back. His bloodshot eyes were focused intently upon Wade. "I'm just thinking about something you said earlier."

"Yeah?" Wade grunted as he separated good junk from the bad. "Like what?"

"Like how Livingston handles his money. I believe you mentioned he hung onto it better than he hung onto his wife."

"Yeah. What about it?"

"It sounds like you may know a lot on that subject."

Wade looked away from what he was doing to look at Clint. He held his stare for only a second or two, which was more than enough for him to let a few things slip.

"I know plenty about it," Wade grumbled. "I've been working for that Englishman for a while now."

"That's not what I mean."

"If there's something you want to say, Adams, just say it."

"All right, then," Clint said as he got to his feet and took a few steps toward Wade. "Let's start with the fact that Livingston got us both in here and blew us up because he was certain one of us slept with his wife. I know for certain it wasn't me."

"Oh, some crazy Englishman decides to toss some dynamite, so that means I must be the cause?"

Rather than say anything to that, Clint simply kept his stare held level upon Wade. It was the same stare that had cracked more than a few good poker players and earned Clint quite a bit of money. It was also the same stare that had saved his life more than a few times.

Wade cracked in about three seconds.

"Fine!" Wade snarled as he kicked the trash in front of him. "I slept with her! Hell, I'm just a man and that cat was in heat from the moment I set foot onto this property. She practically threw herself at me!"

Clint was still staring at him when Wade looked up again.

"I might have done some talking of my own, but she didn't exactly resist," Wade amended. "You ask me, she was probably spreading her legs for half the men in that bunkhouse."

"But none of them got caught."

Wade shook his head and dropped down to sit upon the floor. After kicking another pile of garbage, he leaned back and stared at the jagged rock over his head. "It should just be me down here. It's because of me that you're even in this mess at all, not to mention this damn mine."

"Yeah," Clint said with a chuckle. "You're right about that."

Wade looked over as if he couldn't believe his ears.

"What did you expect me to say?" Rolling his eyes, Clint added, "All I wanted was for you to own up to it. I'm not exactly the one to be preaching about not getting into trouble on account of a woman. I don't even know how many times it's happened. I just have one more question for you."

"What is it?"

"Was she worth it?"

Wade grinned and said, "Oh, yeah, she was." But his smile quickly started to fade as he asked, "Do you think she's really dead?"

"Livingston didn't look like he was in the mood to kid around about it."

"No, he sure didn't. Whether she cheated or not, she didn't deserve to be killed by the likes of him."

"That's all the more reason for us to get out of here and pay him a visit."

Wade nodded slowly and got back to his feet. "Yeah. He should have to pay for what he's done."

"You don't even know the half of what he's done."

Commencing his task of sifting through the old and rusted tools, Wade said, "Go on and explain it to me. Lord knows we've got plenty of time for stories."

TWENTY-NINE

"How long are we going to stand here, sir?"

Livingston sat in his saddle with his hands placed casually upon his knees. As always, he looked more like he was sitting on a throne. With a self-satisfied grin on his face, he said, "We'll sit here until I say it's time to leave."

"It'll be dark soon."

Livingston's royal demeanor slipped a bit as he glanced at the hired gun who had been doing the talking and asked, "Do you think they're dead in there?"

"If the blast didn't kill them, they're sealed up in that mine for good. They had to have gotten injured, which is just as good as a bullet in the head under them circumstances."

"Is that a fact?"

Although the hired gun hadn't worked a mine for a day in his life, he nodded with complete confidence and replied, "It's a fact, sir."

Livingston studied the mine's entrance for a few more seconds. Every time some of the rocks shifted, his heart jumped a bit closer to the roof of his mouth. Over the last few minutes, however, those occasional shifts were growing fewer and farther between.

"Are you certain you used enough explosive?" Livingston asked.

The same gunman nodded. "I guarantee it."

"All right, then. Since this mess is straightened out, it's time to see to the rest of it."

Livingston steered his horse toward home, and the rest of the men were more than willing to follow him.

"Have there been any men trying to cross the fence?"

The oldest of the gunmen answered that one. Unlike the others, he'd been working for Livingston for several years. "Not for some time. It's been pretty quiet."

"Good. Since Walsh is probably expecting to hear from Mr. Adams, we should have at least another day or two of peace and quiet."

"Didn't you send someone to fetch Mr. Walsh?"

"You mean like I told Adams?" Livingston scoffed. "Most certainly not. I was foolish enough to listen to him for a short while, but saw the error of my ways when he was revealed to be a wolf in sheep's clothing."

"You mean one of them was."

"Excuse me?"

The older man riding beside Livingston shrugged and said, "You mean one of them was a wolf, seeing as how one of them . . ." Although he knew exactly what he wanted to say, the ranch hand winced at the thought of actually saying it.

Livingston nodded impatiently. "Yes, yes. Well, I was foolish to have trusted either of them."

"What if one of them is innocent?"

"That doesn't matter anymore, does it? Besides, I listened well enough to Mr. Adams's plan and took enough away to form a fairly good plan for myself. That, coupled with the fact that Walsh is surely waiting around for word from his spy, means that the time is ripe for us to make a strike of our own."

"We've been doing plenty of that, sir," the ranch hand said. "It doesn't seem to be doing much good."

"That's because we've been disorganized and indecisive. I've been far too lenient with that filthy Irish mongrel and the time has come for all that to stop."

Letting out a haggard breath, the ranch hand leaned in close to Livingston and dropped his voice to a whisper. "I've known you for some time, Emmett, and I know the truth between you and Mr. Walsh. Don't you think it's better to find some other—"

"You don't know a damn thing about me and Mr. Walsh," Livingston hissed. "If anything, you know a few lines in a very thick volume, which gives you absolutely no right to judge me."

"Not judging, sir. I was just making sure that—"

"Yes," Livingston said as he looked completely through the ranch hand. "I am very sure." He then turned to one of the newly hired gunmen and said, "I want you to ride ahead and get the others ready. Tomorrow, we'll be taking a stand and ending this once and for all."

"Should we ride armed?"

"Oh, yes," Livingston said with a smile. "There's no sense in riding any other way."

THIRTY

Clint and Wade rattled with every step they took. After looting the trash-strewn cave for everything they could use, they were forced to carry their loot in tattered sacks or hanging off belt loops and shoulder straps. Clint had found an old tin pan, some rusted shovel heads, and several lengths of timber. Wade had found a lantern with a few spoonfuls of oil and a few various pieces of tools for himself.

"I feel like a goddamn transient," Wade said.

"Well, that's good because that's exactly how we look."

"So was all that true about Livingston and Walsh being brothers and all? I mean, are you sure about it?"

Clint was walking behind Wade, but that didn't make the going any easier. For every crack or hole in the tunnel that Wade found, there were plenty of others that were lost in the shadows to twist ankles or snap knees.

"I didn't check through an official family tree," Clint replied. "But I'm pretty certain Walsh wasn't lying. He doesn't have much reason to."

"No, I suppose he doesn't. Still, going after your own brother?" Wade let out a low whistle and shook his head.

"That's a hell of a thing for someone to do. Especially for someone as soft as Livingston."

"How does a man like that make it out here?" Clint wondered. "I've seen men like him try to head out west and wind up dead in a matter of days."

"Probably thanks to his brother," Wade said simply. "Walsh is a hard son of a bitch. That's why I can't see them both coming from the same father."

Clint mulled that over and nodded. "No, but it does explain how Livingston survived out here."

After thinking it over, Wade smirked and said, "Yeah, I guess it does. Good thing I'm along to figure these things out, huh?"

"Yeah," Clint said as he knocked his elbow against the side of the tunnel for what must have been the fiftieth time. "Thanks a lot."

Wade ignored the comment and stretched his arm out in front of him. "You ever done any mining, Adams?"

"A bit."

"You really think you can find your way out of here?"

Clint stepped up alongside Wade and studied the shadows long enough for his eyes to adjust. Between the thick darkness and the bright, crackling torches, both men's eyes were always trying to shift from one extreme to another. "Yeah," he said. "And if you play your cards right, I may just bring you along."

Wade let out one coughing laugh that was loud enough to echo all the way down the tunnel into what sounded like forever. "I'm sorry as hell about all this."

"You didn't blow up that tunnel."

"Yeah, but . . . I kind of caused it. I did sleep with Mrs. Livingston."

"If anything, it forced Mr. Livingston to show his true colors. Even though I'd rather not be stuck in here right now, at least I know who we're dealing with."

"But you don't need to be dealing with any of this."

"I get wrapped up in this sort of thing a lot," Clint admitted. "You might say I've got a good nose for sniffing out trouble."

"That's a good way to stay out of it."

"True. Then maybe I'm just a soft touch." Clint kicked away a foot-long rat that scurried over his boot. "It's about time I did something to fix that."

"That's a load of shit and you know it," Wade said.

"Really? I suppose you learned that when you took my name?"

"No. I learned that when you didn't try to kill me after finding out I took your name. You're a good man, Clint. Unfortunately, the world has a bad habit of chewing up and spitting out good men."

"Yeah. I noticed."

They'd been walking at a steady pace for a while and it was only their instincts that told them they were making any progress whatsoever. Their eyes only saw a never-ending flow of rough tunnel, broken up with cracked beams. Their ears heard the same echoes bouncing off the walls into the distance.

The rats were getting bigger and the flap of leathery wings was getting louder, but those weren't exactly encouraging. Clint and Wade passed the next hour with more idle conversation, and even started swapping bad jokes while taking turns at the front of the line. Finally, Wade stopped and held up his hand.

"Hold it a second."

"What is it?" Clint asked.

"Looks like the tunnel's coming to an end."

Clint felt his heart drop into the pit of his stomach. It sank even lower when he took a look for himself and saw a solid rock wall less than twenty paces in front of them.

"Shit," Wade grunted. "We came all this way and now we got to go back? I don't even recall any turns we missed."

"There's got to be more to this mine," Clint said as he walked forward. "A mine can't just be one tunnel. Can it?"

Both of them held their ground for a few seconds. The truth was they were too afraid of finding out they'd reached the end of a long, newly sealed cave.

"Wait a second," Wade said as he started jogging forward. "I think I see something."

Clint thought he saw something too, but it was just a deep dent in the wall that he'd mistaken for another tunnel. By the time he looked back to Wade, he saw the man turning to his right.

"The tracks go on from here," Wade hollered. "There's a cart!"

Wade started running toward the cart, certain he would find another series of tunnels and several more possibilities for escape. What he found instead was a huge, yawning cavern and the echoing trickle of dripping water.

The tracks beneath his feet extended another few steps before ending abruptly at a few broken wooden planks. Wade tried to stop, but only slid in the loose gravel. When he grabbed onto the cart, he only managed to pull it over the side with him.

THIRTY-ONE

"Holy shit!" Clint shouted as he heard the mix of skidding footsteps and metal grinding upon metal.

His own instinct was to run after Wade, but Clint managed to try and stop just a bit sooner than the one who'd gone before him. When he turned the corner, he saw the tracks reemerge from the collected dust and gravel. It looked as if those tracks had once gone over a wooden bridge that spanned the large open area directly ahead. There was no bridge anymore.

It was a dead end in every sense of the word.

Clint's boots slipped along the gravel and his momentum carried him toward the edge of the broken bridge.

Only then did he hear the jarring sound of something heavy slamming against the floor of the cavern below. As much as he hoped he wouldn't, Clint waited for the pained screams that would surely follow that crunch. What he got wasn't quite what he was expecting.

"Umm . . . how about a little help?" came a squeaking voice amid the distant clatter.

Clint pulled his torch in so he was no longer holding it out into the empty space. Rather than look out, he looked straight down and saw two hands clasped onto the edge of the broken track.

Hanging there like a worm on a hook, Wade swung back and forth from one curved piece of steel track. His fingers were bloody and the rest of him was covered with dirt and rust. Surprisingly enough, he seemed rather calm while gazing up at Clint.

"Lend me a hand?"

Snapping himself out of his surprise at what had happened, Clint set his torch down and dropped to his knees. "Sure, sure. Just hold on, Wade."

Clint reached down to grab hold of Wade's wrists. The man was sweating and covered in dirt, which meant he couldn't have been harder to lift if he was trying. Even as Clint started to lift, he could feel Wade slipping through his fingers.

"I've got you," Clint said. "Just try not to move."

"Clint, you might want to—"

"I said don't move, Wade. You're squirming."

"I know, but you really should look at—"

"Do you want to fall?"

"No!" Wade shouted. "Just look to your right, god-dammit!"

When Clint looked to his right, the first thing he saw was a pair of beady eyes glittering in the shadow against the wall. The next thing he spotted was a set of teeth just beneath those eyes as a huge rat scurried toward his hand.

Clint fought back the instinct to pull back his hand since that was the one that was about to haul Wade up from where he was hanging. Before that thought finished running through his mind, Clint moved his other hand over to take a swipe at the rat before it could sink its teeth into him.

His hand was about to smack away the incoming rodent when it felt as if it had been snagged on a fishhook. He recoiled instinctively and found another rat attached to that hand by its teeth and scratching at his wrist with thorny claws.

Clint gritted his teeth as the sound of more claws scratching against rock closed in around him. Forcing himself to look down at Wade, Clint couldn't help but notice that flinging the second rat over the side and more rats swarming in on him like he was meat on a dinner table.

As he reached out to once again take hold of Wade's wrists in both hands, Clint managed to swipe a few more of the rats kicking and squealing over the side.

"Watch where you're tossing them things!" Wade said.

"Just shut up and take hold of the track."

Pulling back hard enough to feel the strain in every muscle along his back and shoulders, Clint dragged Wade up while craning his neck to keep the hungry rats away from his face. Unfortunately, Wade wasn't in a position to avoid that particular hazard, and was soon high enough to attract a few of the rats away from their main course.

Even as one of the rats tore off a bit of his cheek, Wade managed to find a section of the cart's track that was still firmly anchored to the ground. The timber crossing the iron rails acted as a ladder for him to pull himself up from the side.

Now that Wade was able to get himself back onto solid ground, Clint turned his attention to his own set of problems. For every set of gnashing teeth and scraping claws that he knocked away, two more found a spot to tear into him. The sound of the rats ripping through his clothes and nibbling on his flesh became louder within the cramped tunnel and even began to echo in his ears.

Clint jumped to his feet and took so many of the rats with him that he felt as if he was wearing a heavy fur coat. Not only did the rodents hang onto him, but they even started to climb up along his legs and arms so they could get to the exposed skin of his neck and hands.

Smacking his arm against a wall produced a satisfying

crunch, so Clint repeated the gesture a few more times. He then reached down to grab hold of the torch and do something that went against every shred of his better judgment.

Without a second thought, Clint brought the flaming end of the torch in close to his own body until he could feel the heat of the fire under his shredded clothing. Fortunately, the rats could feel that heat even more and started dropping off him and scurrying away. He then swept the torch along the ground to discourage any of the braver rats from trying their luck.

"Where the hell are these things coming from?" Wade shouted as he nearly fell over the edge again in his haste to shake some of his rats free.

Clint brought his torch closer to Wade, and dazed them enough for them to lose their grip and hit the ground running or fall over the side.

"That's a good question," Clint said as he lowered his torch. "And I think it might just take us another step closer to getting out of here."

THIRTY-TWO

Once he got his footing, Wade was stomping on the remaining rats like he was doing some sort of angry jig. Only after he managed to catch one of the rats squarely under his boot did he stop and savor the moment. When he looked up at Clint, he smiled and nodded proudly.

"What do you want me to do?" Clint asked. "Applaud?"

"For starters, you could stop eyeing me with that torch in your hand."

"Are you hurt?"

"I'm damn lucky that cart didn't roll me over or crush my damn fingers," Wade said as he held up his hands and showed Clint the bloody fingers in question. "But I don't think I'm hurt."

"Anything sprained or broken?"

"Nah."

"Then step aside."

"Real compassionate of you, Adams. Thanks a lot."

"I pulled you up from there, didn't I? Now step aside."

Wade grumbled under his breath, but finally did move so Clint could walk past him. He then started taking inventory of what he'd lost in the fall.

"Dammit," Wade snarled. "That lantern I found is gone!"

Stepping cautiously toward the edge of the broken tracks, Clint hunkered down low and kept the torch about a foot over the ground. "That thing wasn't good for much anyhow. It probably would have gone up in flames the moment you tried to light it."

"Yeah, well, the oil was good for starting torches."

"Didn't you keep some of that oil separate from the lantern?"

"Yeah."

"Do you still have it?"

After patting one of his other pockets, Wade grinned. "I sure do."

"Then put together a torch and come over here."

With the broken bridge right there, finding chunks of wood lying around wasn't a problem. In a minute or so, Wade was dripping some of the oil onto a strip of sackcloth and then wrapping it around the lumber. Clint reached to light the torch, which quickly illuminated the tunnel and sent the few lingering rats scurrying.

"No," Clint said sharply when he saw Wade lift his boot to crush the closest rat. "Let it go."

Although he wasn't happy about it, Wade lowered his boot onto empty ground and let the rat pass. The rodent scampered straight toward the broken rails and dashed between Clint's feet. From there, it turned a corner and disappeared from sight.

. "Stupid rodents," Wade grumbled. "Don't even know better than to run off the side of a cliff."

"Maybe not so stupid," Clint said. "Take a look for yourself."

Clint was leaning out over the side and extending his arm even further. Reluctantly, Wade eased his way to Clint's side until he was practically standing in the same spot where he'd fallen not too long ago. Rather than lean out, Wade looked over Clint's shoulder and held his torch up high.

"That's not as big of a cave as I thought," Wade said.

"Thank God for small favors. Look down here," Clint said as he waved his torch downward.

Wade craned his neck and stretched his legs until he was finally able to see what Clint was trying to show him. "I'll be damned," he said.

Clint's torch threw some light down onto a narrow ledge that wrapped around the corner from the tunnel and extended along the wall before leaving the torch's light. A few rats were still scurrying along that ledge in a single-file line of twitching tails and dirty, wriggling little bodies.

"Guess that answers my question," Wade said as he swung his torch out over the broken rails. "Too bad this gap is too far for us to jump. If we find some rope somewhere, we might be able to climb down."

"We're not going down. We're going across."

"Unless you can jump like a gazelle and toss me as well, we're not going across that broken bridge!"

But Clint wasn't looking at the bridge or the rails. His eyes were still glancing toward the narrow ledge that was, for the moment, free of rats.

"Aw, hell," Wade muttered.

A few minutes ago, Clint was begging to feel some air on his face and be somewhere without a ceiling that was about to cave in on him. Apparently, whoever heard such things had a sense of humor because Clint had now traded them in for a whole new set of pains in his side.

The cavern was big enough that light from the torches was unable to show the top. Also, the cavern felt like more of a natural structure, which felt somewhat less apt to collapse. On the other hand, Clint and Wade were seeing that cavern while pressed up against its side and sidestepping along a ledge that was only slightly wider than their heels.

Clint shuffled out ahead of Wade. He'd tried to keep his torch in hand as he went, but came too close to losing his balance along the way. Therefore, he'd taken to gripping the torch between his teeth so he could stretch both arms out and slide his palms along the wall.

Since there were still a few rats scuttling back and forth along the ledge, Wade wasn't so quick to let go of his torch. He moved at half the speed of Clint and almost slipped twice as much. That way, he could swipe at the ledge with his torch when he saw a furry body running over his boots.

"This is a damn terrible idea, Adams! For all we know these rats could be going into some goddamn hole at the end of this ledge."

"Shut up," Clint said in a voice that was muffled by the torch gripped between his teeth.

Wade kept sliding along the ledge, fighting to keep himself from looking down. Every so often, he lost that battle and glanced at the inky blackness under the ledge. Pulling his head back away from the sight, he knocked his skull against the rock wall behind him and let out a curse.

Clint didn't want to look down, either, but he kept doing so anyway. He was more concerned with figuring out what kind of a drop they were looking at should they slip. Also, if Wade was right about where the rats were coming from, they might just have to jump and hope for a safe landing.

As much as he strained his eyes, Clint couldn't see anything but shadow beneath him. The trickle of water could be heard, but that might be coming from anywhere inside the mine. As for the bottom of the cavern, it might be ten feet down or a hundred.

"Drop your torch, Adams," Wade said as if skipping ahead in Clint's own train of thought. "See how deep that hole is."

"Jus another cou-le ov steds," Clint said around the torch.

"What? Spit that torch out so I can understand you."

Shaking his head, Clint scraped along the wall and kicked away the rats that nipped at his heels.

Wade was several paces behind by now and in no hurry to catch up. "I'd drop my torch, but . . . well . . . one of us needs to keep the light going up here."

Before he could think of a more convincing argument, Wade saw Clint lean to one side and grunt unintelligibly. If he was closer, Wade would have been able to reach out and pull Clint back. As it was, all he could do was watch while Clint stumbled a few more steps and then fell forward face-first.

THIRTY-THREE

Clint felt his footing start to slip, and immediately knew he was about to see the bottom of that cavern the hard way. Only a few heartbeats before that, however, he'd spotted where the ledge widened into a true path. Once he began to fall forward, he pushed off with both feet and stretched his arms out in front of himself.

When he flew through the air toward the end of the ledge, Clint felt as if he was swimming through molasses. Although he'd been certain he could reach the ground he'd spotted, that hope slipped away quickly. The longer it seemed he hung in midair, the more he started to brace for when he started to plummet all the way down.

The ground hit him in the chest like an angry mule. Clint's hands scrambled for a hold and found plenty of ground to grab onto. His legs kicked out into empty air, but that changed as he pulled himself all the way to safety. Once his fingers found the tracks embedded into the ground, he knew he was going to survive.

"Clint! Are you all right?"

Rolling into a seated position, Clint took the torch from his mouth. After the close call he'd just had, it was no easy task to pry his teeth from where they'd dug in. "Yeah," he replied. "I'm fine."

Wade had been leaning forward to see what happened to Clint. Even though he could see the torch Clint was holding, he couldn't see much else. "What's over there?"

"Looks like another tunnel," Clint said as he shifted to look around. After getting to his feet, he took a moment to survey his surroundings. "Yeah. It's another tunnel. Come on over."

Now that Clint was on his feet, Wade shifted his attention back to his own predicament. The moment he looked down, he felt his knees start to buckle. It was a tense couple of yards, but he managed to work his way over to where Clint had jumped without sliding off.

That almost changed when his toe bumped against something in the ledge. Lifting his boot, he saw a deep rut in the rock. It had started out as a crack in the ledge, but had been worn away by hundreds of scampering feet as they rushed to and from a nearby hole in the wall.

"I found where the rats came from," Wade reported.

The light from Clint's torch was already fading as he scouted the next tunnel. "Great," he shouted. "You want to stay there and make friends or are you coming with me?"

Muttering to himself as he stepped over the rats' trail, Wade stopped just short of the next ledge. From there, he could see where the ground widened out again to form a proper walkway. Unfortunately, there was a break in the ledge that left around four or five feet of empty space between himself and the landing.

Sucking in a deep breath, Wade crouched as much as he could and then jumped forward. His boots landed squarely on solid ground, but then promptly skidded out from under him. Wade landed in a heap while shouting loudly enough to fill the whole cavern with a fog of profanity.

"Are you coming?" Clint asked as he poked his head out

from the tunnel. "Or do you need me to pull you along some more?"

Wade shot a deadly look at Clint and climbed to his feet. He took one more look over his shoulder and down into the dark hole behind him. Doing so, he couldn't help but wonder how deep that hole truly was. Rather than satisfy his curiosity, he turned his back to it and walked toward Clint's torch.

"There's some more tools over here," Clint said as soon as he heard Wade's steps closing in behind him.

"More lanterns, too," Wade added, pointing toward a set of posts with rusty lanterns hanging from them by a set of nails.

"Good, because I'm out of matches."

"There's a work station right over there. Might be something we can use inside."

Clint looked over to where Wade was headed. Although he'd glanced in that direction before, Clint thought there was only a large pile of kindling stacked there. On second glance, he could spot a door in the middle of that pile, which somewhat resembled a small shack.

Wade and Clint both walked toward the shack. Their steps echoed more and more the further they went until it was obvious they were coming up to a large, open area. Hearing that was enough to get both men thinking about something other than a leaning shack. They went a little further before stopping dead in their tracks.

The area ahead of them was open, but it was also a twisting labyrinth of intersecting tunnels held up by groaning timber.

"This might take a while," Clint said.

THIRTY-FOUR

Wade was right about a few things. The pile of lumber Clint had spotted was a shack, after all. Not only that, but there were some tools to be found in that shack that were in much better condition than the ones they'd found before.

They'd also managed to salvage three lanterns that actually worked and enough oil from the other lanterns to fill them. Despite their luck in stumbling across all those things, neither one of them was too happy. In fact, they didn't say much of anything for the next hour as they walked back and forth down the intersecting tunnels.

It was Clint's idea to systematically walk every tunnel in search of a path that led them to another exit from the mine. It was also his idea for him and Wade to stick together in case something happened along the way.

Before too much longer, Clint started to regret that last decision.

"I'm hungry," Wade said.

Clint nodded and kept walking.

"Aren't you hungry, Adams?"

Clint ignored the question and kept walking.

Wade sighed and glanced down one passage while Clint checked the opposite one. When they saw just another set of walls leading to another intersection, Wade asked, "Wouldn't a nice, juicy steak hit the mark right about now? A thick steak with mushrooms and some grilled onions. Jesus, I'd kill a man for a steak. Oh! And a beer. What I wouldn't give for—"

"If you don't stop that, I'll make you eat this shovel."

"No need to get mean. I was just thinking about a steak and maybe some apple pie."

Clint stopped and turned on the balls of his feet. "How about if I find a rat and cook him up? Would that keep you quiet?"

"Do you have any mushrooms and grilled onions?"

Letting out an exasperated breath, Clint turned back around and started walking. Suddenly, he grinned and said, "That might not be a bad idea."

"What?"

"Cooking up a rat. They've got meat on their bones, don't they?" As he said that, Clint could almost hear Wade's stomach turning over.

"They're not even worth it," Wade grunted.

"I don't know. Those rats that were crawling on you seemed pretty fat to me."

"I'm not eating a rat."

"But you're so hungry," Clint said. He didn't even have to look over his shoulder to know that Wade was wincing and trying to keep the disgust from showing through in his voice. Just to push him over the edge, Clint added, "What about if we roasted a bunch of them up and smashed them together? Maybe like a sandwich. There should be more than enough grease to keep the whole thing from falling apart."

After that, Clint didn't have to ask again for Wade to keep his mouth shut. They explored the rest of those tunnels quickly and quietly. Standing at the opposite end from where they'd started, Clint and Wade were close to walking every inch of that place before stopping.

"Hold up," Clint said. "I see something."

Wade shifted around and took a look. "Hey, I see it, too! Looks like that tunnel goes on a hell of a lot longer than the rest we've seen."

"It sure does."

"You think it leads out of here?"

"I don't know," Clint admitted. "But it's got to take us one step closer."

Both of them lifted their lanterns and walked slowly toward the tunnel at the far end. Although they wouldn't say as much out loud, neither one of them had the strength to run. Clint's hands were scraped up so badly that the blood formed a crusty paste between him and his torch. His muscles had been screaming for mercy for hours and every one of his joints ached.

Just thinking about any possible wounds was enough to make every last one of them hurt all over again. It wasn't until that moment that Clint truly appreciated all of Wade's constant chatter.

"So you slept with Mrs. Livingston, huh?" Clint asked as a way to get Wade going again.

"Sure. Didn't you?"

"No. I barely even met her. Come to think of it, I can't even recall if I met her."

"She's a fine woman. Tits like ripe melons and legs that were strong enough to crack open a walnut."

"And here I thought you were going to get sentimental," Clint said with a laugh.

They were leaving the intersecting tunnels behind them and moving into newer territory. So far, all they'd seen throughout the tunnels was rusted cart tracks and a few discarded picks. Clint had collected a couple bags as well, but they were empty. Tearing off a shred from one of those bags brought another question into Clint's mind.

"What kind of mine was this supposed to be, anyway?"

"Silver, I think," Wade replied. "Maybe turquoise. Wait

a second. Do you get turquoise from a mine? Eh, it was probably silver, anyway."

"I don't know about you, but I haven't seen anything besides rats and rocks down here."

"I may just have to cook up a few of those critters if we can't—"

Wade stopped talking as if someone had suddenly shut him down.

"Believe me, I'm not looking forward to that any more than you are," Clint replied. When he no longer heard Wade's steps, Clint glanced back at him to find the man on one knee with his ear against the wall.

"What are—?" Clint was cut short by a quickly raised finger, so he shut up and watched to see what Wade would do next.

Finally, Wade looked up at him and asked, "You hear that water?"

"Yeah. I've heard it most of the time we've been down here."

"But it's louder now," Wade said. "And it's coming from that direction."

THIRTY-FIVE

From the moment he stood back up, Wade was eager to run down that tunnel. Clint followed closely behind, keeping his eyes open for holes in the floor or any number of things that could bring a rushed trip through an abandoned mine to a quick stop.

As the tunnel went on, the walls became rougher. Soon, it was obvious that few tools had scraped the sides of the tunnel except to knock in a few hastily crafted posts. Those wooden supports were more like toothpicks meant to hold up one end of a bank vault. If that tunnel decided to come down, there was nothing a few posts could do about it.

Wade didn't seem to mind that one bit as he wove between the posts and even knocked into a few in his haste to make it further into that tunnel. No tracks had been laid down on the ground and no tools were to be found. Which served to make an obvious point.

"This might not be a great idea," Clint said.

"What's the matter, Adams? You getting used to the idea of living down here?"

"Better that than dying down here."

"You know what I mean. Besides, if I made it this far after getting blown up, I ain't about to die from getting wet."

As they walked, Clint and Wade's boots were getting more and more soaked. It had started off as a wet slapping sound when they took a step, but progressed until their feet sloshed in a few inches of water. The posts were becoming more spread apart and the ceiling was getting lower. Soon, they had to duck down to keep from knocking their skulls against the jagged stone ceiling.

"What are you hoping to do here?" Clint asked. "I mean, this tunnel was probably flooded even back when there were men working down here."

"But the water's got to come from somewhere, right?" Wade asked while tapping his head to show that he was putting his brain to good use. "This much water don't just drip off the walls. It's got to be leaking in and if we find that leak, then we should be able to get out."

Although Clint could find plenty of holes in that logic, he kept them to himself. They'd already checked through the last set of tunnels and come up empty except for this one. Since trying his luck at the bottom of that cavern where the tracks had broken didn't appeal to him, Clint figured he might as well let Wade test his theory.

They kept walking down that tunnel and the water kept creeping its way up their legs. Soon, every step they took brought the water up another inch as the ground beneath them sloped more and more. Clint was forced to hold his torch up a little higher so he could keep his arm dry. When he did, he felt his torch smack against the top of the tunnel.

"Looks like this tunnel doesn't go much farther," Clint said.

Wade stooped down and reached beneath the water. "Maybe," he grunted. "Or maybe not."

"We might be able to swim a ways, but I'll bet it won't be long before the top of this tunnel comes all the way down until we won't be able to hold our heads up."

"Maybe we shouldn't hold our heads up."

"Dammit," Clint said. "I knew you were going to say something like that."

"It's either that or retrace our steps, and there's not much back there that we haven't already seen."

"There's the hole we climbed around."

Wade looked at Clint with a scowl etched into his face. "If there was anything worth seeing in that hole, wouldn't the miners have built some ladders heading down there?"

"Maybe they did."

"And maybe you're afraid of getting your hair wet," Wade taunted.

"No, but I am afraid of swimming too far underwater and then drowning. No, wait. That's called common sense."

"This ain't exactly a common circumstance, Adams. We're lucky to have made it this far, but let's not fool ourselves. We don't have any food and there sure as hell ain't gonna be any to find down here. Not with all them rats running around.

"That means we need to get out of here and be real quick about it. If we wait too long, one of us is bound to get hurt and that'll only make things more difficult. Once we start to starve, that won't make it any better, either."

Clint let out a breath and shook his head.

"What's the matter, Adams? You think I don't know what I'm talking about?"

"No, I think you hit the nail on the head. That doesn't mean I have to be happy about it."

Wade chuckled and forged ahead. "I'm not right too often, so I'll just savor the moment."

As Wade moved straight down the tunnel, Clint kept his eyes open for any trace of a tunnel that might branch off from the main one or lead to higher ground. All he saw was a whole lot of spiky rock formations jutting from the ceiling and a few wet rats paddling in the opposite direction.

Clint passed up the opportunity to make a comment about sinking ships and followed Wade.

"Well," Wade said after another few minutes. "Looks like this is it."

Sure enough, the tunnel's ceiling took a sharp downward turn and didn't stop until the rock was no more than an inch or two above the surface of the water. Judging by the echoes of the drips and sloshes as the water slapped against the sides, the tunnel had plenty more to go before it ended completely.

"You're still going on?" Clint asked as he saw Wade hold his lantern as high as he could and enter the deeper water.

"It's coming from somewhere. I just know it. Besides, if I'm wrong, we can always go back and check on that rat hole with the broken tracks. Aren't you coming?"

Clint was tearing off strips of material from the sacks and anything else he'd collected or had on his person. "I am, but we're going to do this the smart way. I know how much that goes against your grain, but just humor me."

THIRTY-SIX

Wade was up to his neck in water so cold that he was already losing some of the feeling in his toes after only a minute or two. Although he usually wasn't the first one to dive off of a rock into a stream or swim to the bottom of a creek to pick up something that might have caught the light, he was more than willing to keep going now.

The main difference this time was that he was convinced this was his only way out. Although the rat hole might have a tunnel or two leading out of it, he would rather take his chances on drowning before heading back into that territory.

Behind him, Clint was standing at a spot where the water was right at chest level. His arms were at the water's surface and he was spooling out the makeshift rope he'd put together from all those strips of canvas and burlap. The other end of the rope was tied to Wade's waist.

"I need to take a dive and see what's down here," Wade shouted.

The words echoed back loudly, like rocks that gained momentum while sliding down the face of a mountain. "How's it look so far?" Clint asked. "You see any other tunnels?"

"Nope. There's a few spots where this one widens out, but I can see the backs of them from here."

"Don't try to go too far on your first dive. And remember to pull on the rope if you get into trouble."

"I will, Pa. Don't you worry."

"I'm serious!"

Wade stared at the jagged wall in front of him. The only light helping him along came from all the lanterns that he and Clint had lit a little ways back. Their light reflected off the water and Wade's eyes were adjusted to the dark well enough to allow him to see the walls around him and a little ways under the water's surface.

At the moment, Wade wouldn't have minded being completely in the dark. At least that way he wouldn't have felt like he was buried alive inside a stone casket that had been tossed into a river. Standing there, Wade did his best to prepare himself for what was to come. The lower half of his body was either numb or halfway there and his heart was slamming like a hammer inside his chest.

Knowing things weren't going to get any better in the next few minutes, Wade filled up his lungs with a big breath and squatted down beneath the water.

Once the water had washed over the top of his head, Wade heard things from every corner of his brain. He heard his uncle making fun of him after his first swimming lesson. He heard Meredith Livingston shouting out as her legs tightened around him. He heard Clint saying what a bad idea this was. He even heard his own voice telling him that he was about to find the way out of that goddamn mine.

After a few seconds, his lungs started to burn and his heart raced. He made the mistake of opening his mouth, allowing the crisp, cold water to flood into him and knock like an icicle against the back of his throat.

The shock of that was enough to make his heart skip, which sent him into a panic.

Wade kicked his legs and flailed his arms, certain that he was about to drown.

His next mistake was straightening both legs in a desperate attempt to get his face above water. Although he succeeded in doing that, he also cracked the top of his head against the jagged rock ceiling. Sucking in a few breaths, Wade felt a warm trickle against his ear and neck. He reached around and dabbed the aching part of his head, sending a sting all the way down to his jaw.

"What happened?" Clint asked. "Are you all right?"

Wade looked at his hand and saw the watered-down blood coating his fingers. When he dabbed it again, the blood was still there, but not enough to cause too much concern. "Yeah, I'm all right." he said. "Just wasn't ready for how cold it was gonna be."

"Just make sure you are ready before you try it again."

Wade looked back at Clint and grinned. "Aw, I didn't know you cared so much about me."

Bending down a bit so he could see Wade's eyes beneath the low-hanging rock, Clint replied, "You're damn right I care. Who would carry all this stuff and test out these hare-brained schemes if you weren't around?"

Turning back around to face the deep water, Wade took a few quick breaths until he felt the blood flowing through him once more. Although he was still a bit shaky, he knew it was best to dive right back in rather than stand where he was and build it all up in his head.

Wade slowly filled his lungs again and dropped straight down beneath the water. This time, he was expecting the cold as well as the strange feeling of being in the dark and under the water. Surprisingly enough, it wasn't half as bad the second time around.

After a second or two under there, he could even see a little ways in front of him. The light reflected under the water, which was cold enough to feel good against his eyes. Either that, or he was even number than he thought.

Wade used his feet to move through the water and his hands to feel what was directly in front of him. The floor was rough enough for him to keep pushing himself along until he felt one side of the wall brush against his shoulder.

Now that he was completely submerged, all Wade could hear was the dull thump of his boots against the floor and the muted scrape of his hands against the walls. Soon, another sound came to him. It was a sound apart from the beating of his heart or the straining of his body as it fought the impulse to pull in a breath.

At first, he thought the sound was a sort of rumble. Then he realized that he was hearing rushing water coming from somewhere up ahead. Either that, or it was water falling into the rest from up above. Either way, Wade knew that spot was where he wanted to be.

Rather than swim all the way back to where he'd started, Wade reached up with one hand and stretched his arm as far as he could. Sure enough, his hand emerged from the water and came up another couple of inches to boot.

He arched his back and slowly straightened his legs until he felt the water fall away from his face. Even then, it took him a bit before he could open his mouth and take a breath. The air rushing into his lungs was one of the best things he'd ever experienced. It was so good that he almost completely missed the tugging of the rope around his waist.

"Hey, Adams! Can you hear me?"

Clint's voice was distant, but clear. "Yeah. What did you find?"

"Sounds like there's something up ahead. I'm going to check it out."

"You've got about another ten or twenty feet of rope left. If you need to go any further than that let me know."

"Will do, Pa," Wade chided.

Even though he'd given Clint a ribbing about all his

fussing with the rope and all, Wade still checked to make sure it was tied securely around his waist. It wasn't much of a rope, but a thick cord that was already stretched to its limit. It did seem to be holding up, however, so Wade thought it could stand up to some more punishment.

He braced himself once more for the slap of cold water against his entire body and pulled in a deep breath before diving under.

The floor was dropping away under his feet, forcing him to kick and paddle with one hand. He kept the other hand stretched out to feel along the walls and over his head. Every now and then, he would bob up and take a look around. Unfortunately, the darkness had swallowed him up and the glow of the lanterns was well behind him.

The sounds were still enveloping him like a bag that had been tied over his head, telling him the ceiling was only a few inches away. Sucking in one more breath, Wade dropped beneath the water and did something he hadn't done for a hell of a long time.

He started to pray.

THIRTY-SEVEN

Even as the rope had spooled out of his hand, Clint was tying on more pieces to the free end of it. He did that until he ran out of things to shred apart from the clothes on his back. Rather than start tearing up his shirt, he thought he'd wait and make sure it was worth the effort.

If Wade couldn't find anything with the rope he'd been given, there probably wasn't much to be found. Either that, or Wade had just enough rope to get himself in way over his head.

Clint knew better than to think ahead to the worst in times like this. Once a man started doing that, things that were already bad seemed that much worse. And if a man saw things as the worst they could be, it made it near impossible to keep fighting.

Despite his intention to stay positive, Clint felt his doubts creeping back in once the rope stopped spooling from his hand. Even though he couldn't see more than a faint glimmer, he stared down into the water. He thought he saw some movement down there, but realized it was just the ripples at the surface playing tricks on his eyes.

"Wade?" he shouted. "Can you hear me?"

Realizing he was still looking into the water, Clint took

a few steps into it and hunched down so he could sight a ways along the surface of the water. "Wade! Answer me!"

Tentatively, Clint tugged on the cord. He didn't feel much resistance, but figured that was because Wade was quite a ways out. Hoping his knots were all strong enough, Clint tugged a bit harder until he did feel the slack run out and the cord draw taut.

Keeping himself hunched over, Clint stared straight ahead and strained his ears to hear beyond the constant slapping of water against the walls and the trickle of it dripping back down.

Other than that, there was nothing.

"Wade!"

Clint's voice bounced off the walls, but faded without so much as a peep in response.

The cord was still taut in his hand and hadn't moved enough to convince him that it was tied to someone trying to swim one way or the other. Letting out a curse that was aimed at himself as much as the situation in general, Clint walked into the water so he could follow in Wade's path.

For a while, Clint was able to move swiftly while feeling the water rise up toward his chin. Before too much longer, he'd gotten so deep that it was getting harder to move his legs. When he did push ahead a few more steps, his boots began to slip against the bottom.

Although he didn't keep pulling on the cord, he did make sure to reel it in as he went. That way, it remained somewhat taut and he could feel if there was anything moving at the end of it. Just as he was about to worry even more, Clint felt a quick tug on the rope.

"Wade! Is that you?"

When he didn't get a reply, Clint sucked in a quick breath and dropped below the water.

The shock of the cold was felt right down to the marrow in his bones. Opening his eyes turned out to be a chore in itself since every instinct he had told him to keep them closed, clench his fists, and tough it out until he could get warm again.

But Clint shoved those instincts to one side and opened his eyes. That was right about the same time that he ran out of breath.

He exploded from the surface and pulled in a breath while forcing himself to keep trudging ahead. The cord was twitching in his hand the way a fishing pole jumped when something took the bait. Even though the light was fading behind him, Clint sucked in a breath and dove again.

There wasn't much to see under the water apart from the grit that his boots had kicked up and the smooth bottom of the tunnel. Clint could pick out a few shapes in the water, but none of them was moving and none was even half of Wade's size.

Rather than head for the surface again, Clint took hold of the cord in both hands and started pulling. He pulled himself through the water much faster than he could have swum. It was also a good way to avoid most of the irregular rock shapes that had been scraping and knocking into him every step of the way.

As Clint moved through the water, he knew he would find Wade one way or the other. Either he would pull himself to the other end of that cord or he would pull Wade to him. Since he was running out of air, Clint just hoped one of those two alternatives would happen real quickly.

Clint pulled once more and felt the struggling at the other end of the cord suddenly stop. He kept pulling while floating through the water until he finally reached the end of the cord.

The only thing at that end was a frayed, shredded strip of burlap.

THIRTY-EIGHT

Clint held that broken rope in his hands and stared at it. In all the shoot-outs he'd survived and all the hell he'd been through, he'd gotten real good at thinking on his feet. This time was different, however. This time, he wasn't even himself.

He'd been rattled by an explosion, been trudging through caves for hours on end, been chewed on by rats, nearly fallen off sheer drops, fumbled in the dark, and been scraped or bruised on every inch of his body. Now, he was all but numbed by the cold water, and might have just lost the closest thing he had for a partner through all of this.

His brain raced, but it seemed to be running in a circle.

He was so tired and worn out that he felt all of it might just go away if he sat down and went to sleep for a moment.

But that was just the fatigue talking.

Clint might have been through a lot, but he knew better than to just give up.

That wasn't even a real option in his book.

Not so long as he could draw a breath.

When he snapped himself out of his fog, only a few seconds had ticked away. Before he lost even one second more, Clint let go of the rope and used both hands to plow

152

through the water. His eyes were wide open and searching for any shape that could possibly be Wade. Even as the light faded to nothing, Clint stretched out with both hands to feel his way along as much of the water as he could.

If Wade had any chance at all, Clint was going to fight for him. They'd both come too far together to die now.

It felt as if he was forcing himself to see through sheer will alone. Part of him knew his eyes were adjusting to the shift in light as well as being underwater, but usually adjusting his eyes didn't hurt that much. The cold lanced through the sockets in his face like daggers, which served to sharpen his senses and resolve even more.

Clint kept pumping his arms and kicking his legs until his hands finally brushed against something that wasn't rock. A few seconds later and he might have missed it altogether. As it was, he barely felt something bump against the side of one arm and reflexively grabbed it.

He could feel Wade's elbow within his grasp, but didn't start celebrating just yet. Wade wasn't moving. He wasn't struggling for air and he wasn't even reacting to Clint tugging at him.

After looping his arm under Wade's, Clint started heading up toward the surface. While reaching up to paddle with his free hand, Clint felt his knuckles smack against jagged rock before they even broke the surface of the water.

He started kicking and paddling back the way he'd come without pausing to think about anything else. Clint didn't even consider the fact that he couldn't see much of anything in the water. He didn't even consider the possibility that he was swimming in the wrong direction.

Clint was running on nothing but instinct. Fortunately, his instinct hadn't gotten him killed just yet.

This time was no exception.

The dim glow of the distant light grew just enough to catch Clint's eye. After a few more frantic kicks, he reached up and felt his hand break through the water. Clint reached down to take hold of Wade's other arm while straining both legs to move them upward.

Clint emerged from the water with a noisy splash and a desperate gasp. His heart slammed against his ribs while his lungs begged for more air. He lifted Wade to the surface and held him there, listening for any sign of life.

"Come on, Wade," Clint said while shaking the other man. "You can't die here. I'm not about to drag your sorry ass all the way out of here."

Wade let out a slow breath, which quickly turned into a heaving choke. After hacking up some water, he was able to tread water well enough without Clint holding him up.

"Wh-what was that?" Wade asked in a haggard voice.

Now that Wade was moving and talking, Clint felt all the strain and panic from the last few moments catch up to him. "I thought that would get a rise out of you."

"Where the hell am I?"

"Not far from where I found you."

It wasn't much, but that seemed to be enough to jog Wade's memory. "Oh, yeah. I must have blacked out."

"What happened? Did you get stuck somewhere?"

Although Clint couldn't see the man's face very well, he could hear the excitement in Wade's voice clear as day.

"Oh! I think I found what I was looking for," Wade said in a rush.

"What did you find?"

"I heard water dripping down from above. The closer I got, I heard it was coming down pretty steady. There's a spot where the top part of the tunnel is cracked. There's water coming from above."

"You mean like a waterfall?" Clint asked.

"Not something that big, but I figure it's at least got to lead to another cavern that's higher up than this one. The rock's pretty thin up top and I was trying to break through. That's when I felt you tugging at the cord. I was just about to crack that rock when I started to get dizzy."

"I guess that's right around when I came looking for you."

Wade shrugged and said, "I heard you shouting for me, but I was so close that I didn't want to stop and answer."

"Or take a breath."

"Yeah . . . well . . . I was so close!"

Clint let out a deep breath, which was enough to get his heart beating at something close to a normal pace. "Tell me where to look and I'll check on what you found."

"What about them tools?" Wade asked. "Where did we leave those tools we collected from around here?"

"They're back in the shallow water. Let's catch our breath, gather those tools, and do some more swimming. You all right to keep going?"

Wade nodded. "I couldn't have been out for long. Otherwise, I'd be in plenty worse shape."

"All right, then. Let's get the hell out of here."

THIRTY-NINE

Clint's head broke the surface of the water and he pulled in a breath. Since he'd been going through those motions for a little while now, they seemed much more natural than when he'd pulled Wade back after the man had almost drowned.

"Did you find it?" Wade asked anxiously.

"Not quite, but I heard it. There's definitely water coming in from somewhere."

"Let me go. I can find it again."

"Just stay put and catch your breath. You can take over once I need a rest."

"Fine. Just follow your ears and swim up to the top of the water. You won't have any space to breathe, but you should be able to find the spot I was talking about."

Rather than waste any more breath talking, Clint nodded and checked the rope around his waist. It was still just a collection of rags knotted together, but a bit shorter since they'd taken out the strips of burlap. That was the material that had ripped before, and Clint didn't want to gamble with it again.

"Here," Wade said as he stretched out a hand. "Take this pick with you."

"Not until I know where I'm going," Clint said. "Otherwise, it'll just be weighing me down."

Even in the almost complete darkness, Clint could see the frustration on Wade's face as he pulled back the pick he'd been offering.

Before Wade could say anything more, Clint pulled in a deep breath and dropped below the water. He didn't even feel the cold any longer, since the portions of his body that hadn't toughened up to it had gone numb. When he swam to the spot that was completely submerged, he kept his eyes shut since his hands and ears were doing all the searching anyway.

When he heard the flow of water grow louder, Clint swam up toward the top. He stretched out both arms until his palms bumped against the smooth rock over his head. Rather than work his way further back, he started going from side to side.

For once, he went against what his instincts were telling him as far as where the source of the water's flow was located. The more he moved around, the more he realized how close he was.

The sound was all around him. Depending on which way he turned his head, it seemed to be coming from a different direction. Right about when he felt his heart grinding to a stop thanks to lack of air, Clint swore he'd found exactly what he was after.

Rather than go all the way back to where Wade was waiting, Clint only went back far enough to get his mouth and nose over the water. As he was indulging in a few more breaths, he felt a tugging at his waist.

"I'm just catching a breath," Clint shouted back.

"Find anything?" Wade asked from the shallower water.

"Almost." Clint dove beneath the surface, and could still hear Wade's muffled voice churning through the water.

This time, instead of searching for a spot, Clint went straight back to the one he'd found earlier. The sounds were the same, and he even recognized the pattern of swirls that had been molded into the rock after countless years of contact with the water.

Clint placed both hands flat against the rock. His eyes snapped open in surprise when he found exactly what Wade had said he would find. He still couldn't see it, but Clint could feel a crack in the rock that was as long as his forearm and just a bit wider than his little finger.

Pushing his fingers up into the crack, Clint found himself pulling at it as if he could tear the rock apart with his bare hands. His fingertips wedged into the crack just enough for him to feel something close to a stone blade at the end of a tomahawk.

What surprised Clint the most was that a chunk of that stone actually did snap loose beneath his insistent fingers. After that first chunk snapped free, Clint was able to reach his hand up just a little further into the crack. He managed to get his fingers all the way in, right up to the knuckles. When he bent them, Clint could feel that even more of the rock was practically as thin as the edge.

Even though he was short on breath, Clint kept pulling at the edge of the rock. Although he didn't widen the crack with every attempt, he could hear the rock creaking and straining like ice that was about to break. Every groan and creak he heard made him want to try harder until he had both hands stuck into the crack and had both feet flat against the surface of the rock.

Clint resembled a fly on a ceiling as he kicked and pulled at that crack. It wasn't until he started to see bright colors floating in front of him that he realized just how badly he needed to take a breath. But even when he felt his lungs start to burn, Clint didn't want to give up.

To make matters worse, Clint saw a faint beam of light coming from above after he managed to blink away some of the spots. It didn't occur to him that the light was coming from the nerves in his eyes straining from lack of air.

Clint swore he could break through that rock and swim past it if he just kicked and pulled a bit more.

He could imagine the wide-open tunnel on the other side.

He knew there had to be plenty of ways out if he could just break through that flimsy crust of rock separating one chamber from the other.

Once he got through that rock, it had to be a short walk into the fresh air and everything would be just fine.

Then, he thought back to Wade's limp body floating near this very spot. Clint imagined this was what had to be going through Wade's mind when he had blacked out and almost died.

Clint didn't know how long he'd struggled or how long his chest felt like it was about to bust open. He couldn't even recall the last couple of seconds.

The blobs of color were gone and it felt like he was floating up through empty air.

That's when he felt the insistent tugging at his waist.

FORTY

"Come on, come on," Wade said as he planted his feet and used both hands to grip onto the rope.

It seemed like hours since he'd started tugging on that rope. Not long ago, he'd graduated to hauling on the rope with all his strength. He waited for the moment when he would feel that rope snap, and had already planned where he would swim if that happened.

But the rope didn't snap. In fact, as he started pulling, Wade could feel something heavy being dragged in along with it. Walking back through the shoulder-deep water while straining every last muscle in his arms and back, Wade hauled the rope in until he saw a dark shape bob to the surface.

That shape was still for a long moment, but soon started flailing in the water before finally flipping over. Clint gasped wildly and reached out with both arms.

"I found it!" Clint gasped. "I found it. I was just about to break through!"

"Take a breath first," Wade said as he dragged Clint into some water that was shallow enough for him to stand or even sit without going under. When he took Clint's hand to drag him a little farther, Wade felt the warm blood seeping from Clint's fingers. "Jesus, you weren't kidding."

Clint was breathing steadily now, sucking in the air to fill his greedy lungs. "I know right where it is. Give me a pick and I should be able to widen the hole enough for us to get through."

"I've been thinking about that," Wade said. "We don't know what's on the other side of that hole or how far it is to the top. It might lead into a bigger cave that's filled with water and neither one of us could make it out."

Clint shook his head and blinked quickly. When he spoke this time, there wasn't as much desperation in his voice. "We've got to give it a try. I mean, that's what we were looking for."

Wade was quiet for a moment before nodding. "You're right. But we can't stay under that long or one of us will kill ourselves. We need to take it easy and chip away at it slowly."

"Either that," Clint said, "or both of us can swim down there and break through it in half the time."

Wade studied Clint's face as if he could truly make out every detail in the thick darkness. "Are you still short a few breaths, Adams?"

Clint shook his head. "Every time we head down into that water, we're weaker than the time before. I know we can break through it, and together we both might be able to crack it in one shot. If we can't, we can head back and try it your way."

"All right then," Wade said as he picked up two of the smaller picks and handed one over to Clint. "After you."

They didn't have any trouble finding the spot they were after because the water was churning loudly compared to the trickle that it had been earlier. When they saw and heard that churning, Clint and Wade raced to that spot as if they were a pair of seals instead of two tired men with picks in their hands.

As they kicked to the top, both of them were already swinging their picks up toward the source of that churning water. The first few strikes merely scratched against the rock, but Clint's pick struck the edge of the opening and widened it easily.

Rather than try to swing at it again, Wade felt for the fissure and stuck the pick all the way in. From there, he twisted it so the pick was wedged in there snugly.

When Clint saw Wade's handle protruding from the ceiling, he took that same idea and copied it. As the seconds ticked away and they both started to feel the ache of their lungs, both men propped their feet against the top of the cave and pulled on their pick handles with every bit of strength they had.

Whether it was due to the constant scratching of both men or the decades of erosion from the water, the rock had been whittled down to a thin shell. All it took was one concentrated effort, and both Clint and Wade found their arms swinging backward as their picks came loose.

Clint dropped his pick as he felt his entire body get pulled up through the broken shell of rock. His ribs scraped against the jagged stone, which made a loud crunching sound in his water-filled ears. Despite that, he reached up with both hands and kicked his legs to try and reach the top of the water before his vision blacked out completely.

Just as his boots scraped past the broken rock, Clint began to feel dizzy. More and more, it seemed as if he was standing back and watching himself kick and thrash in the water instead of actually going through those motions himself.

All he could see was blackness and all he could hear was the slowing beat of his heart.

When he felt the cold against his hands, Clint thought

he'd knocked against yet another rock wall. When his head popped up from the water, he barely even recognized the feel of air blowing across his face. There was no mistaking the smell of fresh air, however.

Smelling that air might have been one of the best moments in Clint's life.

The sky above him was dark, but it still felt like he was staring into the face of the sun. What little light there was sent a jolting pain through Clint's head, but it was easily overshadowed by the sound of wind blowing and grass rustling nearby.

Before he could savor the moment for too long, Clint felt something knock against the bottom of his feet and then against the backs of his legs. Once he'd moved aside, Clint saw a familiar shape explode from beneath the water.

"Holy shit!" Wade said with a wheezing exhale. "We made it!"

"Yeah, we sure did."

Both men looked up and around as their eyes adjusted. They expected to find a waterfall, a larger cave, or even a tower of rocks over their heads. What they found was a rough stretch of land with a creek running swiftly through it.

Clint and Wade were sitting in the middle of that creek.

FORTY-ONE

"I gotta tell ya," Wade said as he shifted around to look back and forth over either shoulder. "This ain't what I was expecting."

"It sure wasn't," Clint agreed. But when he took in his surroundings a bit more, things fit into place a little better.

They'd emerged from the bottom of the creek at a spot just below where the water flowed over a large patch of rocks. The water moved just fast enough to make noise as it flowed into a spot that was slightly wider than the rest. From there, it flowed on along a meandering path that disappeared into the distance.

All things considered, it was a fairly nice little creek. At least, it had been nice before it spit up the two filthy, battered figures that only now started to get their feet beneath them.

The water level had dropped considerably, leaving a wide ring of mud around the creek's small basin. The crack in the bottom of the basin could be felt, and even strained beneath Clint and Wade's combined weight. Both men crawled out of the water and onto dry land. Once there, they flopped onto their backs and looked up at the stars.

They lay there, enjoying the fresh air for a while before either of them said a word.

"Near as I can figure," Wade said amid a series of hacking coughs, "this creek must've been right over the mine and dripped through. How long you think it's been draining?"

"Long enough to make that river in the mine," Clint replied.

"I'll be damned. You really think so?"

"It's a good enough explanation for me. I'm more concerned with figuring out where we are."

Wade stood up and looked around. He squinted hard at something on the other side of the creek and said, "We're just over the fence on Mr. Walsh's side."

"How can you be so sure?"

"See those trees over there? The ones that look like hangman's trees? They're on the wrong side of that fence compared to how I'm used to seeing them."

Clint spotted the trees and then spotted the fence just beyond them.

"Yep," Wade grunted. "I know right where we are. I've patrolled this goddamn fence long enough to see all of it in my sleep."

"Think you can get us to Mr. Walsh's house?"

"I'm not so familiar with his land, but I should be able to get to the middle of it."

"That should be good enough. Let's get moving while we still have some wind in our sails."

"Speak for yourself," Wade muttered. "I used up the last of my wind crawling up from the bottom of that lake."

Clint looked over to the creek and then back at Wade. "Lake? Looks more like a puddle to me. Only you would be tired after getting out from there."

At first, Wade was going to say something to defend himself. When he looked back at the basin behind him, though, he could only let out a tired laugh. "That thing is pretty pathetic," he said while studying the creek. "Kind of hard to believe that connects to the river we both nearly died in."

"You nearly died," Clint said as he got to his feet. "I had a momentary lack of breath."

Wade stood and dusted himself off. He then picked a direction and started walking. "Jesus Christ. Remind me again why I even bothered trying to save your life."

"Because you had to repay me for saving yours. By the way, you still owe me one."

"The hell I do!"

It wasn't the most intellectual conversation he'd ever had, but it was enough to keep Clint going long enough to spot the houses in the middle of Walsh's property. Without something to occupy his mind, Clint would have had too much time to think back to all the swimming, walking, running, and climbing he'd done in the last couple hours. In that time, there hadn't been any time to rest. By now, it was sheer will and a distracted mind that kept Clint upright.

Judging by the occasional stagger and weariness in his voice, Wade was in the same boat. By the time they snuck around to the back of Walsh's house, both men were having a hard time keeping their eyes open. They were in such ragged shape that neither one of the men saw the figure walking straight toward them until it was too late.

FORTY-TWO

"Who's there?" came a voice in the darkness just ahead of Clint and Wade. "Show yourselves or I'll scream for help."

Clint stepped forward and squinted at the figure that was cautiously backing away. It was a figure that he most definitely recognized. "Claudia?"

She stopped backing up, but didn't come any closer. "Who are you? How do you know my name?"

"Claudia, it's me. Clint Adams."

She leaned forward and took a step toward him. After a few seconds, she pulled in a surprised breath and rushed at him with her arms open wide. "Oh, my God, I heard you were dead!"

Even though he liked the feel of her arms wrapped around him, Clint was nearly knocked off his feet. "Almost, Claudia, but not quite."

After giving him another hug, she held him at arm's length and looked him up and down. "What happened to you? And what are you doing with him?"

"Hello, Claudia," Wade said as he took a step forward. "You're a sight for sore eyes."

Focusing solely on Clint, she whispered, "He's one of

Livingston's gunmen. I've got a gun in my pocket if you need it."

"It's all right. He was in all the hot water I was in. Of course, he was the main reason for the fire to be set under us in the first place."

"Tell me what happened."

"In a bit," Clint said. "First of all, I need you to get us some horses. We have to get onto Walsh's property."

"You are on his property," she said matter-of-factly.

"Then what are you doing here? I know I'm still rattled, but you worked for Livingston the last I checked."

Even in the dark, Clint could see the expression that came over Claudia's face. Just hearing the Englishman's name was almost enough to make her spit. "That bastard killed his wife. Did you know about that?"

"I heard as much, but didn't know if I could believe it."

Wade stepped forward and stared directly into Claudia's eyes. "Meredith's dead? You're certain?"

She nodded and put Clint between herself and him. "He threw her down the stairs," she said. "The whole house heard it. I was cleaning one of the bedrooms when I heard it. I rushed out to look and saw him run down after her. I thought he was going to help her, but he . . . he just left her there to die."

"Jesus," Wade said. "I thought the Englishman was bluffing."

"He's riding over here to try and clean this place out."

"What?" Clint asked.

Claudia nodded. "He came back bragging about how he killed Meredith and then you two. Since then, he's been getting all his men together and armed them to the teeth. That's when me and a bunch of others ran off."

"You and how many others?"

"At least a dozen. Mostly just workers and folks that were hired on before all this turned so crazy. But a few of the hired guns came along as well. Not many, but enough to hold Mr. Livingston up for a bit."

"So you and the rest came over here?"

"There was nowhere else for us to go. Mr. Walsh was nice enough to take us in. Some say he's just holding us as hostages, but at least we're out of the line of fire."

"So what were you doing out here now?" Wade asked. "Thinking twice about crossing Livingston?"

Claudia shook her head defiantly. "I was watching to see if anyone else was trying to come along with me. There have been a few here and there, running this way after jumping the fence, but I've heard a few gunshots as well. Mr. Livingston said he would shoot anyone that tried to leave, so I guess he's following through on that."

"Son of a bitch," Wade said in disbelief. "I never thought that Englishman had it in him to turn into a mad dog."

"After his first taste of blood," Clint said gravely, "the rest becomes a whole lot easier."

Wrapping her arms around Clint, Claudia said, "I'm just glad you're not dead. After hearing what Mr. Livingston said, I thought there was no way I'd ever see you again."

"He came awfully close, but we managed somehow." Although Clint held Claudia in his arms, he was looking around on all sides. "Is there someplace we can hole up? We need some rest and food."

"And a doctor," Claudia added as she stepped back to get a more careful look at him.

Wade shrugged and waved that off. "No doctor. Just some food."

"I'd like to see Mr. Walsh," Clint said. "But it might not be a good idea for Mr. Walsh to see Wade just yet."

"Are you sure you can trust him?" she asked.

"Yes," Clint replied without hesitation.

"Then come on." Claudia took Clint by the hand and started jogging toward one of three small buildings in the distance. "Mr. Walsh is letting me and the others stay in his old servants' quarters. It's not much, but there are a few separate rooms. Your friend might have to convince someone to let him stay there, but you've got a room with me, Clint."

Clint looked over to Wade and got an immediate smirk in return.

"Go on," Wade said. "I wouldn't have even looked back if I was you."

Claudia led them to the buildings, which were small and flat enough to have blended in with the horizon upon first glance. The main house wasn't too far away, but far enough for the servants' quarters to have a good amount of privacy.

Although there were plenty of signs of life, the quarters were dead quiet. A few windows were lit, but there was hardly any movement behind them. Clint swore the entire place was holding its breath.

It felt like the calm just before a war.

FORTY-THREE

Claudia slipped into her room and closed the door behind her. Clint was already in there and lowering himself onto the bed. Even though it wasn't much more than a cot, it felt like he was lying on a cloud.

"You sure that other one will be all right?" she asked.

"Wade? He can handle himself just fine."

"I don't trust him. He was passing himself off as you, you know."

"Yeah. I know." Letting out a strained breath, Clint eased back until his head found the threadbare pillow. "He was just trying to get a job."

"So you agree with what he did?"

"No, but he's proven himself well enough."

Rolling her eyes, Claudia could tell that she wasn't going to get much more out of him where Wade was concerned. Actually, she didn't really want to hear much more about Wade. Instead, she sat down upon the bed and ran her hand over Clint's chest.

He winced almost immediately.

"You sure you don't need a doctor?" she asked.

Clint nodded. "I'm feeling better already. What are you doing?"

"Unbuttoning your shirt," she said with a grin. "If you intend on sleeping on my bed, you'll have to do it without these filthy rags you're wearing."

She peeled the clothes off Clint without getting more than a few grunts and groans for a protest. When she had him down to his bare essentials, she took a rag from a washbasin and started rubbing it on him.

"Please," Clint said. "I just need to sleep. I'll change the sheets later."

"Almost done. You feel more cold than dirty now that those clothes are gone."

"I took one hell of a long bath." When he felt Claudia's hands start to rub him harder, Clint nearly yelled out. But the pain subsided as she slowly worked the kinks out of his muscles. "Good Lord, that's nice."

"Roll over."

He did what he was told and stretched out on the bed with his belly against the mattress and his face on the pillow. Soon, he felt her crawl on top of him and start to massage his back and shoulders. The weight of her body at the base of his spine was enough to make him sigh contentedly.

For the next several minutes, she rubbed his muscles and even scratched his back. She stopped for a little bit and then got to work on his sides.

"If I didn't know any better," Clint said into the pillow, "I'd have thought I died and went to heaven."

She laughed softly and then said, "Roll over."

Although he was reluctant for his back massage to end, Clint was anxious to see what she could do for his front. He got the answer to that question when he settled on his back and opened his eyes to find Claudia naked and straddling him.

"Now I do think I'm in heaven," Clint said.

Lifting herself up a bit, Claudia slipped her hands between Clint's legs and started rubbing his inner thighs. "I truly am glad to see you alive," she whispered while easing her hands closer to his growing erection. "With all that's going on, I'm glad to have a moment like this."

"If I have anything to say about it," Clint replied as he reached up to cup her firm breasts, "it'll be several moments."

Smiling, Claudia took hold of his penis and guided it between her legs. She lowered herself slowly down, taking him all the way inside her. She let out a slow breath and leaned her head back, savoring the way he filled her up.

Clint slid his hands along the front of her body and then took hold of her hips. When he began to shift slowly beneath her, Clint felt her body respond almost immediately. Claudia rocked back and forth on top of him, moaning under her breath as she felt his cock become even more rigid inside her.

As she found her rhythm, Claudia started to breathe heavier and move a little faster. Soon, she moved on nothing but instinct as she thrust her hips back and forth until Clint found the perfect spot inside her. As soon as that happened, she shuddered and clenched tightly around him.

After all he'd been through recently, seeing Claudia on top of him was like a dream. Her skin felt smooth as silk and her muscles tightened as she drew closer to her first small orgasm. Clint pumped his hips just enough to push her over the edge and felt her entire body respond to the movements.

When Claudia leaned back to catch her breath, her nipples were hard and her breasts shook as the pleasure kept jumping to different spots under her flesh. Opening her eyes, she looked down at Clint with a warm smile.

Placing her hands upon his chest, she lowered herself down and slid her hands up to the back of his head. "Just lay back and relax," she whispered directly into his ear. "Let me take care of you."

Claudia's breath was hot against his skin. It felt like the first real taste of warmth he'd had in years. The more she rocked on top of him, the easier it was for him to forget about trudging through the darkness in that mine. When she shifted her weight to ride him from a different angle, Clint almost forgot his own name.

After pulling her legs up under her, Claudia set her feet on either side of him and supported herself with her hands flat upon his midsection. From there, Claudia squatted on top of him and bobbed her hips straight up and down. She shook out her hair so it fell over her shoulders and tickled Clint's skin when she leaned forward just a little bit more.

Clint arched his own back now and drove up into her. Claudia slid up and down along his penis with a quickening pace. Whenever he would add a thrust of his own, Clint could feel her fingernails dig into him just enough to heighten the pleasure.

Finally, Clint let out a few short groans. She rode him even harder, urging him on with the movements of her hips as well as the soft words she whispered to him. After another few seconds, Clint felt so good that he would have gone through those mines four more times just to get into that bed with her.

Judging by the exhausted smile on Claudia's face, she felt the same.

FORTY-FOUR

Clint woke up to find himself in an empty bed. When he heard the thunder of approaching hooves beating against the ground outside, his first instinct was to jump out from under the covers. That motion was more than enough to remind him of the strain his body was still feeling.

The room was small enough for him to take it in with one glance. Apart from the bed, a small table, and a washbasin, it was empty. His clothes were piled neatly against the wall under the only window. That way, Clint could take a hard look outside while he got dressed.

The sun was just over the horizon in a clear blue sky. Although he couldn't see the horses that were making the noise, he could see plenty of people running back and forth while pointing to the east. Clint buckled on his gun belt and quickly snapped open the Colt's cylinder.

After plucking one round free from its chamber, he lifted the bullet to his eye while rolling it between thumb and forefinger. Just as he'd suspected, there was still a bit of water inside the bullet. Mostly, he could tell by the smell of the powder inside the round, but he knew enough about packing bullet casings to know when something wasn't right inside them.

After dumping out the rounds inside his Colt, Clint replaced them with fresh ones and left the room. He knew the gun needed a good cleaning, but he didn't have time. The rest of the building was full of people either trying to get into their rooms or running out of them. Clint headed for the main door of the small building, but ran into Claudia just before he got there.

"Clint, I was just about to come get you," she said breathlessly.

"What's going on?"

"A whole bunch of riders jumped the fence and are headed this way. There's been shooting and I think some men were killed. All of the horses are headed straight for Mr. Walsh's house."

"Damn. I should have gone to see him before any of this happened."

"There wasn't anything you could have told him that he didn't already know," Claudia replied. "He's been getting ready for this for a while. This place is more like a fort than a ranch."

When he stepped outside, Clint saw the truth in her statement. The night before, all he'd seen was the same boundary fence that had been there the last time. Now, he could see that ditches had been dug behind new fences close to the house where gunmen were able to lie and use the cross beams to steady their aim.

Clint could only see a dozen or so men taking positions behind the fences and half that number riding on horses toward the incoming attackers.

"That you, Adams?"

Clint looked toward the voice, immediately recognizing the man who'd spoken. "Yes, it is, Mr. Walsh."

"I heard you were dead."

"Livingston made a good try of it, but I managed to come out all right. I suppose our plan never saw the light of day?"

Walsh let out a single, grunting laugh. "You kidding? When I never heard back from you, I figured Emmett had gotten over on you somehow. Since then, I've been hoping for the best, but preparing for the worst."

"Well, it looks like the worst is headed straight for you."

"I didn't need to hear that from you. Three of my men were gunned down right at the property line as my brother hopped the fence. He's pulled plenty of underhanded bullshit, but never an outright assault. I never thought he'd go so far."

"Did you hear about what he did to his wife?"

"Yes. It's why I got a shack full of his former employees right now. He loved that woman. I guess he's finally just lost his mind. You don't need to get tangled up in this anymore, Adams. You look like hell, so why not just collect your horse and skin out before hell breaks loose?"

"You've got my horse?"

Walsh nodded. "He came back here wearing an empty saddle. That's another thing that made me think you'd seen your last day."

"I'll collect him and be on my way," Clint said. "But not until after this thing's played itself out. I've been through enough hell already not to turn away from a bit more."

"All right, then. I don't have the time to talk sense into you." With that, Walsh held his hand out and took a rifle from one of his men. "If I don't make it through this, you can collect that fee we talked about from any man here. They know you're to be trusted."

But Clint wasn't worried about collecting any fee. Instead, he was more concerned with the row of men approaching on horseback like a band of guerrilla raiders.

There were nine men that Clint could see. There had undoubtedly been more of them at the start of their ride because these men were either too fearless or stupid to pay any mind to the guns being fired at them. Walsh's men started firing as soon as they could see them instead of when the horses were in range. The riders answered in kind, resulting in a whole lot of sound and fury that signified nothing.

Bullets whipped through the air and fell short of their mark. Since he could judge a weapon's range with a quick glance, Clint kept walking forward without firing a shot. The men that didn't know any better looked at him like he was deflecting the bullets with his teeth. If he made it through this, Clint knew he'd hear this story recounted in a saloon somewhere.

He looked around to see any signs that he was standing up for the wrong side in this fight. His gut told him he wasn't, and that was confirmed when he saw the men huddled behind their fences and only pulling their triggers in earnest when the riders' shots started getting close.

The horses were bearing down on them, and were quickly joined by a few that exploded from a nearby stable. Walsh's riders charged forward and fired off a few quick rounds into the sky. All of Livingston's men shifted their aim until they saw one of the riders closest to them fall from his saddle.

By now, the attackers were close enough for Walsh's men to hit them. One of the lead horses whinnied and reared on its hind legs as hot lead drilled through its flesh. The rider fell from the saddle and rolled to one side before he was stomped to death. One of the men behind Walsh's fences looked to see if that rider was all right and got a bullet through the skull for his troubles.

Another rider was gunned down by one of Walsh's men who thundered toward him on horseback and squeezed off a lucky shot. With the lead still flying, Livingston's horses trampled the closest fence. Upon orders from one of the men who was hanging back, those riders stayed in that spot and trampled a few of Walsh's men under their hooves.

"Kill them all!" Livingston shouted as he sat in his saddle like a field general.

Walsh and two of his men stood their ground and started firing toward Livingston. Compared to Livingston, Walsh looked like a peasant determined to defend his land.

That was all Clint needed to see.

He walked straight through the crowd toward Livingston, knowing that the Englishman was one of the linchpins of this whole mess.

After firing a shot into the chest of another of Walsh's men, one of Livingston's riders turned his sights toward Clint. Before he could squeeze his trigger, Clint's arm flashed up and sent him straight to hell. His horse took off running as soon as it had lost its rider.

Clint kept walking in his straight line.

It was obvious that the men here were the last group of guns that either side had left. A few shots cracked from the fences, but a good portion of those men had already been trampled. As far as that was concerned, all but four of the attacking riders had been dropped, which didn't include Livingston and his two personal guards.

One of the riders thundered up to Clint with a gun blazing in each hand. He let out a feral scream as he pulled both guns toward Clint. Without flinching, Clint turned on his heels, raised his arm, and sent a round over the horse's head and into the chest of its rider.

That man still had a wild look on his face as he was knocked straight over the horse's rump. He landed like a sack of hammers with both fists still wrapped tightly around his guns. He took that feral look of his to the grave.

Only one of the riders remained. Since there were only a couple men still bearing arms on Walsh's behalf, Livingston and his two guards rode closer.

"Time to sign over your property," Livingston said. "Either that, or I'll be forced to kill you and then claim it just like Father would have wanted."

"You leave my father out of this," Walsh snarled. "He'd

spit in your face if he was alive to see this. He'd probably spit in both our faces. Lord knows we've earned it."

"But he isn't here," Livingston said. "The good news is that you'll be joining him very soon." With that, Livingston snapped his fingers and sent his two guards forward.

Wade was the guard to Livingston's right.

FORTY-FIVE

"You can't do this," Walsh said. "Even if you go through me, someone will bring the law down on you."

"You ask anyone along on this whole ride," Livingston replied as he raised his arms to show that he wasn't wearing a holster, "and they'll tell you I didn't fire a shot."

The last rider and one of the guards walked straight up to Walsh with their guns drawn. When they heard Livingston snap his fingers, they took aim and squeezed their triggers.

Two shots ripped through the air so quickly that they sounded like one. The rider and guard each caught a bullet through the forehead, which dropped them so fast that they were sure to arrive in the Promised Land with confused looks on their faces.

Clint stepped forward while shifting his smoking Colt toward Livingston. "You want to finish this? Then do it yourself."

Livingston looked almost in shock. He saw a reassuring nod from Wade as the gunman swung down from his saddle. Livingston followed suit and stood slightly behind Wade.

"There's a mine that cuts through both our properties,"

181

Livingston said. "The entrance is on my land, so sign over your interest in it and we'll be through."

"After all the blood you spilled, you still want an easy way out?" Walsh said. "Go to hell."

"Here," Wade said as he drew his gun and handed it over to Livingston. "Just finish this and be done with it." Before he was even through saying that, he'd drawn another pistol from his holster and aimed it at Clint.

Livingston took the gun and held it as if he didn't know which end was to be pointed in which direction. After pulling in a breath, he raised the gun, aimed it at Walsh, and sighted down the barrel.

"You'd kill your own flesh and blood?" Walsh asked, allowing his own gun arm to hang limp at his side.

For a few moments, the Englishman didn't say a word. Then, after a little shrug, he pulled his trigger.

—*clack*—

Walsh stepped forward slowly so he could yank the gun from Livingston's hand. "You make me sick."

"What?" Livingston groaned as he was collared by a few of Walsh's men and dragged away. "I don't understand."

Grinning, Wade walked past the Irishman and reclaimed his gun. Looking over to Livingston, he said, "I guess my powder got wet when you stranded me in that fucking mine. At least the rest of the world got a chance to see what a miserable prick you are."

"Get him out of my sight," Walsh said to his men.

The hired guns dragged Livingston away without being too gentle about it. That only left Clint, Walsh, Wade, and a few of Walsh's men.

"Much obliged to you," Walsh said to Clint as he stuck out his hand. "I'll see to that payment, but I don't see how that can be nearly enough to show my thanks."

"You can show your thanks by letting me take your brother to the law. He'll hang for what he's done, so just let the proper authorities get their hands dirty for a change."

Walsh's eyes narrowed as he said, "I should be the one to tend to this."

"Enough's enough. Wrap this up properly or you'll regret it for the rest of your life."

Slowly, Walsh lowered his eyes and nodded. "You're right. At least let me arrange for an escort. Oh, and I'm sure you'll want that fine horse of yours back as well."

"I'd appreciate it." After Walsh had gone, Clint looked over to Wade. The gunman was grinning from ear to ear. "Why didn't you tell me you were going back to pay Livingston a visit?"

"Because I knew you'd just talk me out of it. Besides, I wasn't intending on making it a social call at first. When I saw I was just in time to get in on Livingston's little invasion, I knew the only way to stop this thing was to have both brothers look each other square in the eye and lay their cards on the table.

"I couldn't get Livingston to call off his attack, but I managed to get in close to him and put some ideas in his head. I was surprised how easy it was to get him to leave his own gun at home."

"How'd you get Livingston to trust you?" Clint asked.

To that, Wade smiled even wider. He stuck his hand in his pocket and when he took it out, it was filled with rough chunks of dirty silver. "I gathered these up while we were in that mine. All I needed to do was show them to Livingston, tell him I was the only one who knew where to find it, and that greedy little devil was ready to hire me on."

"And he didn't care about you and his wife?"

"I told him you were the one who slept with her and he was in the proper frame of mind to believe me." When he saw the look on Clint's face, Wade shrugged. "Desperate times and all that, Adams! It worked, didn't it?"

"Yeah, I suppose it did. I'm heading off once I get my horse and the money Walsh owes me. What about you?"

Once again, Wade held out the silver in his hand and

then stuffed it back into his pocket. "I think I'll stay here. Working this property might still have some merit."

Clint tipped his hat and walked over to take Eclipse's reins from the kid leading him out of the stable. Before he got too far, he heard Wade call his name. When he turned around, something glittered through the air toward him. Clint snatched the large chunk of silver Wade had thrown.

"You're entitled to a decent share of whatever comes from that mine," Wade said, "The only hitch is that you need to stop by from time to time to collect. Not a bad deal for a couple of middlemen."

Clint held onto the silver and waved. "The drinks will be on you. Oh, and if you pass my name off as yours again, this middleman will kick the hell out of you."

"Fair enough."

Watch for

DANGEROUS CARGO

297th novel in the exciting GUNSMITH series
from Jove

Coming in September!

J. R. ROBERTS

THE GUNSMITH

Available wherever books are sold or at
penguin.com

♩ **GIANT ACTION! GIANT ADVENTURE!**

THE Gunsmith

GIANT

Giant Westerns featuring The Gunsmith

Little Sureshot and the Wild West Show
0-515-13851-7

Dead Weight
0-515-14028-7

Available in October 2006:
Red Mountain
0-515-14206-9

Available wherever books are sold or at penguin.com